SJ Owens is a retired civil servant who lives in Cardiff; she's married with four children, eight grandchildren, and two crazy Springer Spaniels.

SJ always felt she had book "inside her" and believes that you should write about what you know, so her first novel draws on her family's Italian heritage.

SJ Owens

A MOMENT

AUSTIN MACAULEY PUBLISHERS™
LONDON * CAMBRIDGE * NEW YORK * SHARJAH

Copyright © SJ Owens 2024

The right of SJ Owens to be identified as author of this work has been asserted by the author in accordance with sections 77 and 78 of the Copyright, Designs and Patents Act 1988.

All rights reserved. No part of this publication may be reproduced, stored in a retrieval system, or transmitted in any form or by any means, electronic, mechanical, photocopying, recording, or otherwise, without the prior permission of the publishers.

Any person who commits any unauthorised act in relation to this publication may be liable to criminal prosecution and civil claims for damages.

This is a work of fiction. Names, characters, businesses, places, events, locales, and incidents are either the products of the author's imagination or used in a fictitious manner. Any resemblance to actual persons, living or dead, or actual events is purely coincidental.

A CIP catalogue record for this title is available from the British Library.

ISBN 9781035871452 (Paperback)
ISBN 9781035871469 (ePub e-book)

www.austinmacauley.com

First Published 2024
Austin Macauley Publishers Ltd®
1 Canada Square
Canary Wharf
London
E14 5AA

Chapter 1

There are times in a person's life, when they know something has happened which will change their life forever. This was one of those times. As Lianne Reynolds stared out of the bedroom window, she knew that nothing would ever be the same again.

It was early March and the sun was shining. Out in the street there were various people going about their business—parents walking their children home from school; workmen replacing the windows in number 42; and dogs being walked to and from the gardens that ran down the centre of this Victorian road, with its three storey terraced houses.

Outside the window, life continued, unaware of what had unfolded in the front bedroom of number 15.

Lianne sat quietly holding her Mam's hand; it was already cold, despite Lianne's attempts to keep it warm. Her Mam's face seemed somehow peaceful and there was an air of serenity in the room, which was suddenly shattered by the sound of the doorbell ringing. Lianne let go of her Mam's hand and went to answer it.

"Thank you so much for coming Dr Richards," she said, as he walked into the passageway.

"I just wish it was in happier circumstances," he replied, before asking, "Mam upstairs?" Lianne nodded and followed Dr Richards upstairs to the large front bedroom, where her mother lay.

Dr Richards did a few basic checks before confirming what she already knew, her mother had passed away. "There's no rush," he said, "call the undertaker when you're ready. I have some information here for you on what you need to do now, but it's all fairly straight forward. Do you have someone who could come and be with you? I know we knew your Mam wouldn't last much longer, but it's still a shock."

"No, but I'm fine. Thank you, Dr Richards, I think I'd rather be on my own." With that, the doctor left the room, making his way downstairs, as Lianne sat down in the chair that she'd occupied for the last week. Her life as she knew it was over.

Lianne had been an only child; she'd never known her father and her Mam never spoke about him. She would get upset every time Lianne asked about her dad, and so Lianne stopped asking. For the last 29 years, it had been Lianne and her Mam; the dynamic duo, they jokingly called themselves. They had done almost everything together. Whether it was going clothes shopping or to the cinema.

Margaret was not just Lianne's Mam; she was her best friend too. Lianne had talked to her about so many things over the years, knowing her Mam would never judge her and would always give her honest opinion. When she had been in school, Lianne's friends had envied the relationship she had had with her Mam; she could literally ask her anything and Lianne cringed when she thought back to some of the things, she had asked her Mam to explain!

Lianne sat beside the bed holding her Mam's hand for a little longer, but there seemed little point in prolonging the inevitable. Lianne telephoned the undertaker her Mam had chosen several months beforehand, and they said they would be with her within the hour. It had been quite surreal talking to her Mam about her funeral, but Margaret had had quite definite ideas about what she wanted and what she did not want. So she had ensured that Lianne knew what that was, and had already paid.

It was typical of her Mam, Lianne thought, to plan her own funeral as if she was hosting a party. Margaret was always very matter of fact about things and nothing seemed to phase her, not even her terminal diagnosis. What had started as a few slurred words and tripping over a little more than usual, had turned out to be Motor Neurone Disease. Both mother and daughter had noticed the first signs that something was wrong, but neither had thought it was anything to worry about.

However, it had been one such 'trip' over a kerb stone and a nasty cut on her knee that had led to a trip to A&E, and ultimately the diagnosis. The nurse in A&E had commented on Mam's speech, and asked when she'd had her stroke. Lianne had replied, that she hadn't had a stroke as far as she was aware, but the fact that the nurse had picked up on it, meant that Lianne started thinking.

Margaret saw her GP a few weeks later, and he too said, that she could very well have had a minor stroke without really being aware of anything having happened and so he would refer her to the hospital. What followed, was a series of hospital visits to see various consultants, and then, at the age of 45, Margaret had her diagnosis and was told that she had a year, maybe two.

Margaret had been very matter of fact when she told Lianne that evening. Lianne hadn't gone to the hospital with her Mam, as she'd been busy in work, and as far as they were both concerned, it was a fairly straight forward appointment with the consultant that day. Having concluded that Margaret had not had a stroke, the next possible diagnosis had been Bell's palsy; Lianne had 'googled' it. And as both, she and Margaret were very relaxed at the possibility of such a diagnosis, Margaret had insisted that she could go to the hospital on her own, and Lianne need not take any more time off work.

Margaret tried not to show any emotion when she told Lianne what the consultant had said, but Lianne heard her crying in her room later that night and on many more occasions after that.

Lianne had moved back home just 8 months before, when her relationship with Grant had broken down. As she lay in bed that night, unable to sleep, it almost seemed as if it was fate. Once her Mam had gone to bed, Lianne too had headed to her room, but with her iPad, in order to Google MND. She'd been horrified at what she'd found out about this awful disease that would ultimately take her Mam away from her, it was impossible to even imagine what was going to happen. How she would lose the ability to eat and speak, how her muscles would stop responding, leaving her unable to walk more than a few steps, if she was lucky.

And as Lianne listened to her Mam's tears finally subside, her own had started to fall and she sobbed quietly, until she too finally fell into a restless sleep.

When her alarm went off the next morning, Lianne honestly felt as if she hadn't slept at all and when she looked at her reflection in the bathroom mirror, her face looked ravaged and her eyes were red and swollen. She showered as usual, but decided against washing her hair, she just couldn't be bothered. Afterwards, she applied a little more makeup than usual, trying to conceal the effects of the night before. She shoved her hair up with a clip, grabbed a cup of coffee and a piece of toast, which she ate as she shoved her bits and pieces in her bag, and by 7:45 a.m., she was ready to leave the house.

Her Mam was obviously still asleep, so she quickly scribbled a note, which she left on the kitchen table, then headed out of the front door, and into her battered old Clio. The car had been a present from her Mam when she'd started University, and it had already had a good few miles on the clock. It was a tatty old thing, but it was hers, and she had resisted when Grant had kept on at her to change it after she had qualified.

"Why on earth don't you just get rid of the blasted thing?" He'd said, for the umpteenth time, when it failed to start on the first few attempts. "It's not as if you can't afford a decent car," he added, with that edge to his voice, that he always had when he talked about money. He'd always resented the fact that Lianne had got a first and had inevitably landed the better job; it had grated on him that a girl had done better than him, and the fact that it was 'his girl' just made things a whole lot worse.

Grant had been used to being in demand, he'd been the guy all the girls had wanted to go out with in school. He'd had the looks and physique, girls seemed to love so, getting a date had never proved to be a problem. When he went to university, that trend continued, and there was a long list of girls who he'd dated, slept with, and then dumped. Each new girlfriend would be convinced that she was the one to tame him, she'd be the one he'd really fall in love with, and want to stay with, but of course, it never happened that way. Grant would tire of each one quite quickly and they'd be consigned to the list of exes who'd never kept hold of him.

Lianne had been different; she was there to study not to socialise. She knew how hard she had worked to get a place and she had no intention of taking that for granted. She also knew how hard her Mam had worked to get her through school, and how hard she continued to work just to keep a roof over their heads. Grant hadn't taken much notice of Lianne during their first year, he was too busy having a good time, but the novelty soon wore off, and by the start of the second year, he knew he'd have to knuckle down and do some work, or else his parents would cut his allowance.

He sat at the next table to her in the library one cold November evening. He noticed her long, dark-brown, hair which fell across her shoulders, as she leaned over her books. There were three or four on the table in front of her, and he saw her slender arms as they reached across books, her fingers flicking through the pages as she tried to find what she wanted. She never once looked up; she was in her own private world and never saw Grant.

Over the next few days, Grant became intrigued by what he saw; she really was a beautiful woman with her dark hair and olive complexion. She never seemed to wear makeup and was always in jeans and a t—shirt, but there was something about her that drew Grant in. He found himself going to the library more often in the hope that he'd see her. When he finally did, he went over and introduced himself, asking if she'd finished with one of the text books that lay closed on the table in front. She'd looked up and smiled, her hazel eyes seemed to smile too, as she handed him the book.

Grant was used to women noticing him and maintaining eye contact, but not Lianne, her eyes went straight back down and she returned to her studies. Over the following weeks, Grant found numerous reasons to talk to her, in the canteen or the library, and he desperately wanted to ask her out, but something was stopping him and he had no idea what that was.

It wasn't until after the Christmas break that he finally asked her if she'd like to go for a drink, but she politely declined and it took several more attempts before she agreed. It was not until the start of Year 3, that they became a couple, but they both enjoyed some 'me' time too. They moved in different circles and Grant would inevitably end up going out in the evenings with his mates, while Lianne worked into the early hours, as she poured over her books and worked on her assignments. So, as the final exams approached, it was Lianne who felt prepared, while Grant panicked.

The rest, as they say, was history. Lianne came out with a first, whilst Grant had to settle for a two. He managed to get a job, but it wasn't what he'd hoped for. Meanwhile, Lianne got a good job, which meant she could help out financially at home. As far as Lianne was concerned, her Mam had worked several jobs to get her through university, now Lianne had the opportunity to repay her. Enabling her Mam to give up her evening job.

Within a year, Lianne and Grant had decided to move in together. They rented a lovely 2-bedroomed apartment overlooking the bay, but Lianne continued to pay her Mam rent every month, even though she wasn't living at home any longer. She could afford it, and she wanted to pay her Mam back for everything she'd done for her.

Life was good. Lianne loved her job and she and Grant had a good social life. All their friends were people she had met through Grant, but that wasn't a problem; they would regularly meet up for drinks or a meal and always had a great time. Grant would go to the gym several evenings a week, and when he did, Lianne would go over to see her Mam.

They had always been so close, that Lianne couldn't bear to not see her Mam every few days; they spoke on the phone every day, but nothing could replace having a proper catch and a chat with Mam. Grant was the complete opposite; he rarely saw his parents, and Lianne had only met them on a handful of occasions in all the time they had been together.

After about a year living together, the cracks in their relationship started to show. Grant seemed to resent anytime Lianne spent with her Mam and he refused to do any of the housework, even though they both worked full time. His idea of cooking dinner was ordering a takeaway and he had no qualms in complaining to Lianne, if his shirts weren't washed, ironed and hanging up in his wardrobe. Eventually, it got to the point, where Lianne felt she was getting absolutely nothing from their relationship; she knew she didn't want to spend the rest of her life with this man, and she certainly couldn't contemplate having children with him.

When she told him it was over, he swore blind that he would change, that he would do more around the flat, but she pointed out to him that she had been saying so for months, that things needed to change and they hadn't, why would it be any different now? After that, his mood turned to one of anger and he told her to leave. She felt like telling him to go, just to make the point that she had as much right to stay in the flat as he did, but she really couldn't be bothered. Within a few days, she had moved all her stuff out and had gone back to live with Mam; she never saw him again.

Chapter 2

The next few days passed in a blur, as Lianne made all the necessary arrangements for her Mam's funeral. She went to formally register the death, and was grateful for the system in place, which meant that once the death was recorded, any Government department that her Mam had had dealings with, would be notified automatically. That would make things a lot easier and would reduce the number of times she had to tell people that her Mam had gone.

Lianne then met the priest, who would conduct the service in the Church and the crematorium. Lianne contacted the few members of the family that there were; her Mam had been an only child, so the only family were a couple of cousins, and there were the few friends her Mam had had.

Lianne booked a small room in a hotel, close to the crematorium for the wake, and arranged for a few sandwiches to be serve along with tea and cake. The hotel bar would be open, so people could have something stronger if they wanted.

The day of the funeral was one of those glorious spring days, that happened so rarely; the sky was blue with a light breeze and just a few fluffy white clouds. At Mam's request, Lianne wore a beautiful coral and navy coloured shift dress; Lianne's Mam loved bright colours and was adamant that her funeral should be seen as a celebration of her life, so she had specifically asked, that mourners wear something bright and cheerful, not black.

There were about 30 people at the funeral, more than Lianne had expected, really. As well as Margaret's few cousins, there were some of her friends there, a few colleagues from work, and even some neighbours; even a few of Lianne's friends were there to show their support. All in all, things went well and Lianne had managed to maintain her composure, even when she'd delivered the eulogy. She spoke about the type of person her Mam had been, the strength she'd shown throughout her illness and how she had been such an amazing mother.

However, when the curtains closed around the willow coffin adorned with freesias and roses—Margaret's favourite flowers—Li was overwhelmed. At that point, it all became very real and the tears flowed, but as one of Margaret's favourite hymns was played, Lianne composed herself and walked outside into the bright sunshine. At the wake in a nearby hotel, Lianne did as was expected, talking to those who had attended, as they drank tea and ate cake, although afterwards, she had no recollection of anything that had been said.

By the time Lianne got back home late that afternoon, she was exhausted, it was as if she had finally given herself permission to stop and get off the carousel that had been her life for the last few months. She changed into her favourite pyjamas and curled up on the settee with her mum's dressing gown, which still had that familiar smell of soap. That scent she had known since she was a child, which symbolised familiarity and safety. The tears began to flow again, and when she was all cried out, she fell into a deep sleep, still clutching onto the fleecy cloth.

A few days later, Lianne decided to make a start, clearing out cupboards and drawers. Her Mam had made a Will when she found out she was ill, it was very straightforward—everything went to Lianne. The Insurance would cover the remainder of the small mortgage, that Margaret had taken out some 5 or 6 years ago, to do some work on the property. The house would be put in Lianne's name. She didn't know what she wanted to do with it yet, it was a big old house, probably too big for one person, but it was home and she had decided not to make any decisions, until everything had settled down. But there was no reason why she couldn't start clearing out some of her Mam's things.

Some may have thought it was too soon to be sorting things out, but Lianne was very practical like her Mam. Indeed, Margaret had started to clear out a lot of stuff before she had become too ill to get around, she hadn't wanted to leave Lianne to wade through all her stuff. She had filled several large bags with clothes that could go to the charity shop, she lived in a few pairs of comfy trousers, with either a t-shirt or a jumper in those final months, and had no more use for fancy tops and high heeled shoes.

And so, there wasn't too much stuff for Lianne to go through, just a few bits in her Mam's wardrobe and some paperwork, although again, Margaret had been very practical and organised. It was as Lianne finished emptying the wardrobe, that she saw a wooden box at the back on the top shelf. It looked like a beautiful old jewellery box and Lianne didn't recall having seen it before. She carefully lifted it down, and wiped off the dust to reveal the lid, which was inset with various kinds of wood in a swirling pattern. It really was stunning, and Lianne knew she had never seen the box before, but it had obviously meant something to her Mam.

Lianne sat on her Mam's bed and slowly lifted the lid on the box, not knowing what she would find. The first thing she saw was a photo of her Mam, she looked about 15 or 16 and was wearing a pair of white shorts with a bright coral coloured top that accentuated her tanned skin. She was smiling from ear to ear; one of those smiles, that said, 'I am so happy, I could burst'. Lianne had never seen the photo before, and it made her smile to see her Mam so happy.

Turning the photograph over, it said, 'Lucca 1989', Lianne had no idea where Lucca was, so she pulled out her phone from her jeans pocket and googled it. Lucca—it turned out—was a city in Tuscany, Italy on the Serchio river. Famous for its 'well preserved Renaissance walls and cobbled streets'. Lianne continued to browse through various images that Google had come up with; it really was a beautiful place. Yet, her Mam had never mentioned going to Lucca or even to Italy, which Lianne found rather odd.

Lianne went back to looking through the other bits and pieces that were in the box, there was a lovely coral coloured bracelet that Lianne had never seen her mum wear, and lots of photos, all taken at about the same time. Some were of a young, dark-haired man on his own, and in others, the young man had his arms around Margaret, they both seemed so very happy. They were all dated 1989 and the young man was called Alfonso. It would appear, judging by the heart shaped squiggles around the words, 'Maggie and Alfonso' this must have been a holiday romance.

As well as the photos, Lianne found a diary that her Mam had kept from 1989 and as she flicked through the pages, she saw her Mam's familiar hand writing. There were also about a dozen or so letters tied together with a lilac ribbon; Lianne put them to one side, she couldn't bring herself to read them or her Mam's diary, it seemed like an invasion of her Mam's privacy, and she wasn't ready to do that yet. She put everything back in the box, which she then put back in the wardrobe, she was obviously thinking 'out of sight, out of mind' but it didn't work that way, and the next morning Lianne woke from a troubled night's sleep, unable to think of anything else.

Chapter 3

After breakfast, Lianne jumped in the shower; she was just drying her hair, when her phone rang, it was Diane, one of her Mam's cousins.

"Hi Diane," she said, as she answered the call, "I was just about to ring you!"

"Oh dear, that sounds ominous," Diane replied in a light-hearted way, "what have I done now?"

"Nothing," Lianne said. "I found some stuff of Mam's which I've never seen before, and I was hoping you could go through it with me. Could I pop over to see you sometime?"

"Of course, you can, you don't need to ask. When would you want to come over?"

"Are you free today? I know it's short notice, but I've had stuff going through my head all night, and I need to know what it is that I've found."

"Come on over whenever you're ready," Diane said. "I don't have any plans today."

"Thank you," Lianne replied and then added. "Oh, I'm so sorry I never even asked why you were ringing!"

"Only ringing to see how you were," Diane said. "Nothing more than that. So you get yourself over here, and we'll go through what you've found."

Lianne thanked her again and hung up. She had the strangest feeling that Diane knew exactly what she'd found.

Lianne finished getting dressed and dried her hair. She took the wooden box from the wardrobe and put it in a bag, before placing it on the front seat of the car, as she started the 20-minute drive to Diane's.

Diane was her Mam's cousin on her father's side; she'd never known her grandparents, but vaguely remembered Diane's parents. In fact, Lianne knew very little about her grandparents, other than the fact that they had been killed in a car accident before she was born. Diane was a good 10 years older than her Mam, and her parents had both passed away a few years beforehand.

Diane was a widow with three grown up children, who had given her four grandchildren so far, with another one on the way.

As Lianne pulled up outside Diane's house, she felt quite sick; Diane had been the closest to Margaret, and if anyone knew the truth about what she'd found, it would be Diane. As she switched off the engine, she saw that Diane had already opened the front door and was waiting for her.

Lianne walked up the driveway and straight into Diane's arms. Which enveloped her with a warmth and peace, that she hadn't felt for a long time.

Diane led Lianne into the kitchen where the kettle had already boiled. She made them both a coffee and then sat at the kitchen table, alongside Lianne, who had unwrapped the box and placed it in front of her.

"I think I know what I've found," Lianne said. "But if anyone knows the truth, then it's you."

Diane opened the box and took out the photos and the letters; she smiled as she saw the pictures of Margaret, and she knew immediately what it was. Diane sighed as she looked at the photos of 'Maggie and Alfonso', she took a deep breath and started at the beginning.

Chapter 4

Maggie was an only child, and as much as she loved her parents, she felt as if they were smothering her. If she went to meet friends, her dad always dropped her off and collected her later. She was 16 years old, and found it so embarrassing.

"I can catch the bus, Dad, please! There's no need to take me," she said for the umpteenth time, and as always, the answer was no. She was only allowed to go out, if her dad took her, and so half an hour later, her dad dropped her at her best-friend's house. Maggie and Jayne had known each other since infant school and they told each other everything. Jayne's parents were a lot more liberal in their attitudes, so she had considerably more freedom than Lianne. That evening they were heading to the park to meet a group of friends, although Maggie's dad didn't know that. He thought they were going to be listening to music in the house until he collected Lianne at 9:00 p.m.

As the girls walked to the park, Jayne said she had some really exciting news.

"Dad has to go to Italy for a couple of months," she said. "Something to do with his job, I think. Anyway, Mum and I are going out there for the whole of the summer holidays, and Mum said I can take a friend!"

Jayne sounded so excited as she continued, "So will you come with me? It'll be amazing—Dad's being put up in a villa in Lucca with its own swimming pool, so we'll be staying there. Please, please, please say you'll come with me." Jayne pleaded.

Maggie squealed with delight; it would be incredible to go to Italy. She had never been abroad, her parent's idea of a holiday, was a week in a guest house in Torquay! But as she was about to say yes, she suddenly thought of her parents; they'd never let her go and she said so to Jayne. "You know what they're like, they'll never agree to it. It's so unfair."

"Do you want to come?"

"Of course, I do! I just don't think my parents are going to agree. And there's the cost, it's just not going to happen."

"Leave it to me," said Jayne.

A few days later, Jayne's mum rang Maggie's. She explained about the trip and said she was worried that Jayne would be bored stuck in the villa with no friends. Her husband's firm was paying for the flights, etc, so Maggie would just need a little pocket money. Maggie's mum agreed to discuss it with her husband, and Maggie could hardly believe it, when her parents said she could go. She would need a passport and some new clothes, but they weren't going for a couple of months, so they had plenty of time.

Maggie literally shrieked with excitement as she rang Jayne. "I can come," she said, "I can come!"

The girls spent another 20 minutes on the phone. Talking about everything they were going to do and what they needed to take. Maggie still couldn't believe it, and she kissed and hugged both her parents, as she headed up to her room. Her parents weren't the demonstrative type, they rarely made any physical contact with Maggie or each other. In fact, Maggie often wondered how her mother had ever gotten pregnant in the first place.

"Enough of that," said her dad. "We will be expecting you to be on your best behaviour, we don't want any nonsense," he added. "It's very kind of John and Carol to offer to take you, so I don't want to hear that they have had to discipline you, do you understand?"

"I do, Dad, I promise I will behave," Maggie replied, as she bounded up the stairs.

Jayne and Maggie spent the next few weeks discussing everything to do with their holiday—the clothes they'd wear, the makeup they would need, the boys they would meet, etc, etc. When Maggie's passport came through just a week before, they were due to leave, it all started to feel very real.

The big day arrived and Maggie could barely contain her excitement, although she was also terrified at the prospect of flying. She didn't say anything to Jayne, but inside, her stomach was doing somersaults. As the plane finally left the runway, Maggie was even more terrified. She had no idea how the big metal construction, that was packed with people and their luggage had got off the ground, but she just prayed that it would stay there.

A few hours later, they arrived in Italy, and Jayne's father was waiting for them in the arrivals hall. He helped carry all the suitcases to the car, and both girls were enthralled by what they saw. About 30 minutes later, they arrived at the driveway leading to the villa.

It was a glorious day and the villa was stunning; its whitewash walls stood out against the blue sky, and there was beautiful fuchsia-pink bougainvillea trailed across what appeared to be an outdoor dining room! Maggie had never seen anything so beautiful in all her life; it was as if she had been transported to another world.

Jayne's mum interrupted her thoughts, and told the girls to go and unpack their things. She then told Maggie she should ring her parents to let them know she'd arrived safely, which she duly did. She was so excited by everything she saw that nothing could dampen her enthusiasm, not even her parents' reminder that there was to be 'no nonsense'.

The girls spent the next few days around the pool; soaking up the sunshine and enjoying the occasional dip in the water to cool off. Despite the fact that they were together 24 hours of the day, they always had plenty to talk about.

That evening, over dinner, Jayne's mum said she was planning to go into Lucca the following day and she asked the girls if they wanted to go with her.

"I have plenty of things I need to do, but I thought you could both have a wander around the city and do some sightseeing. We'd go in with your dad when he drives to work, and then come home with him in the evening, so you'd have the whole day to yourselves." The girls both agreed. It sounded like fun, especially if they'd have some time to themselves.

They spent the evening discussing what to wear into Lucca and were both up early, to shower and dress for their day out.

Lucca really was a beautiful place, and after agreeing where and when they would meet up with Jayne's parents for the drive back, they set off. They picked up a tourist map and sat on a bench to plan where they were going to go. Their intention was to check out as many Italian dress shops as they could, but they soon found themselves wandering through small side streets that were filled with sights and smells that overwhelmed their senses. After a couple of hours of walking in sandals that were 'the height of fashion', but not very comfortable, the girls were exhausted and saw what appeared to be an ice-cream parlour. They had had breakfast early, so decided ice-cream would be perfect.

They took a seat at a small table on the pavement in front of the shop, and a few moments later, a dark-haired, young man appeared to take their order. His English was almost non-existent and their Italian was even worse; the poor lad seemed really embarrassed when he couldn't understand them, but another guy appeared, who spoke some English and they managed to explain what they wanted.

"You excuse my friend," he said, as he wrote down their order. "He not see such beautiful ladies before!" The girls both laughed and Maggie's cheeks were flushed. When he came back with their ice creams, Jayne started chatting to the guy whose name was Gino, as Maggie sat quietly. She could see the first lad in the shop and every now and then, he would look directly at her, there was something about him that made her stomach do somersaults and she felt herself blush even more.

His name was Alfonso, and Gino said that they were cousins. Gino's father owned the ice-cream parlour and Alfonso had come to stay for the summer and help out. Jayne explained that they were there for the summer too, and that they were staying on the outskirts of Lucca with her parents.

Within a few minutes, Gino's father was yelling at him in Italian, from the doorway. "Sorry," Gino said. "I work. You come back 3 o'clock? I finish work." Gino left the girls to their ice-creams, although Jayne wasn't eating much, she was too busy going on about how handsome Gino was, and wouldn't it be amazing if they had Italian boyfriends! Maggie didn't answer; she didn't get a chance to, Jayne carried on singing Gino's praises, barely pausing for breath.

Eventually the girls left, and headed off again, to wander around Lucca for another few hours, until it was 3:00 p.m. Jayne had it all planned, they weren't due to meet her parents until, 5:00 p.m., so they had plenty of time. They wandered through the numerous shops that were full of colourful gifts, designed to entice you in and spend your Lira. Maggie had never seen so many beautiful things, but her parents had given her little money, so she couldn't afford to buy everything she liked.

However, there was a beautiful coral coloured bracelet in the one shop, and Maggie decided she would buy it the next time she came to Lucca, if it was still there.

At 2:55 p.m., the girls were waiting across the road from the ice-cream parlour, and the boys appeared a few moments later. The four of them started walking, and Gino put his arm around Jayne's shoulder as he led them down toward the river. Maggie and Alfonso fell in behind, and unlike Jayne and Gino, who were talking non-stop, they said nothing to each other, until they arrived at a large park. The four of them sat on the grass and Alfonso looked at Maggie in a way that sent her stomach somersaulting again. "Me, Alfonso," he said and then pointed at her.

"Maggie," she replied.

"Maggie," he repeated, with his soft Italian accent and Maggie felt herself blush.

Jayne and Gino were chatting away, Jayne was laughing at all his little jokes and she faked embarrassment, as he told her how beautiful English women were. Jayne tried to explain that they were Welsh rather than English, but he didn't seem to grasp the difference! Before they knew it, it was 4:30 p.m. and Maggie told Jayne that they needed to go, she didn't want them to be late, although she knew Jayne's parents were not as strict as her own.

"I see you again," Gino asked "You come tomorrow?" With that Alfonso said something to Gino in Italian who responded in English to Jayne. "Sunday," he said. "You come Sunday!" Jayne said she would do her best, and that they would be at the Church of San Michele at 11:00 a.m. if they could get away.

Gino lent in and kissed Jayne very gently on the lips, poor Alfonso, looked terrified, not knowing what to do, Maggie didn't either. So, she held out her hand which he took, but rather than shaking her hand, as she had expected, he had kissed it very tenderly saying, "Addio, Maggie."

The girls made their way back to where they had agreed to meet Jayne's parents, chattering non-stop about what had happened that afternoon. "Probably best if we don't mention Gino and Alfonso to my folks," Jayne said, as they arrived at the meeting point. They were a little early, and Jayne knew that would earn them a few brownie points. "But how are we going to possibly get away on Sunday, if we don't tell them about the boys?"

"Leave it to me." Came the reply.

When they arrived back at the villa, Jayne's mum announced that they were going to have barbecue that evening and that she would call the girls when it was ready. "Would you like us to do the salads?" Jayne asked "Maggie makes a lovely pasta salad, don't you Maggie?" Maggie nodded, not knowing what to say, she'd never made a pasta salad in her life!

"Well, thank you," Carol said. "Why don't you girls sort all that out now, while I have a shower, and then we won't get in each other's way." With that, she headed upstairs and the girls went into the kitchen. Somehow, they managed to cobble together a couple of salads and Carol looked genuinely pleased when she came back down later.

"Your Dad's going to start up the barbecue now, so why don't you two go and shower and change. By the time you've finished, the meat will be cooked." The girls headed up to their room and reappeared about 45 minutes later with freshly washed hair. The food was ready, so the four of them sat at the table on the patio and enjoyed their evening meal as they watched the sun go down. John and Carol had had a few glasses of wine by then, and Jayne decided it was the right time to raise the subject of Sunday.

"Mum," she said, not waiting for a response. "I don't know if you remember, but Maggie is Catholic, so she'd like to go to church on Sunday." Without pausing for breath, she continued, "we saw a beautiful church in Lucca today, so I thought maybe she could go there and I would go with her to keep her company. Then afterwards, we wanted to go to one of the museums, as we didn't manage to see everything today."

"Oh, right, sorry Maggie, I hadn't realised," came the reply. "Of course, you must go to church, we could drop them in couldn't we John?"

"Yes, we can, of course, we can. What time is the service?"

"At 11:00 a.m." Jayne replied, "so we would need to be there about quarter to, if that's OK."

"No problem at all," said John.

"Thank you, Dad. Come on Maggie, our turn to do the washing up," said Jayne, and with that, the girls cleared the table and headed for the kitchen.

Maggie could barely believe how brazen Jayne had been. Yes, Maggie was Catholic, but she honestly couldn't remember the last time she'd been to church. Somehow, Jayne had managed to get them a free pass to go into Lucca on Sunday; she couldn't quite believe it. With that, Maggie realised that Jayne was speaking to her.

"Sorry, what did you say?" Maggie asked.

"I was asking you what you were going to wear on Sunday. Honestly Maggie, I thought you'd be a bit more excited!"

With that, Jayne finished washing the dishes and after Maggie had wiped the last few, the girls headed for their room. The rest of the evening was spent trying on various outfits and 'make up tips' from one of Carol's women's magazines.

The next few days passed quickly, and Jayne rarely spoke about anything other than Gino. How handsome he was, what good English he spoke, what would it be like to be married to an Italian man. The list went on and on. Maggie on the other hand, said little, she felt guilty about having lied to Jayne's parents and couldn't understand why the thought of seeing Alfonso again was tying her stomach up in knots. She had never experienced anything like it; she'd liked a few boys in school, but none had made her feel like this, she almost felt nauseous.

Sunday morning arrived, and John dropped the girls into Lucca arranging to pick them up later. The girls headed for the Church, and arrived in plenty of time. But to their surprise, Gino and Alfonso were already there, and the latter seemed to be as nervous as Maggie felt.

Gino suggested that they walked and they headed for the central plaza. Gino had once again put his arm around Jayne, and Maggie and Alfonso fell in behind them. They carried on walking until they reached the park where they had been earlier in the week and they settled on the grass under the shade of one of the many trees.

Jayne and Gino were chatting away, whilst Maggie and Alfonso sat in silence; she felt very self-conscious and didn't know what to do. She was trying to think of something to say to him, when he said very quietly "You very beautiful Maggie." She immediately blushed, and just as quietly she thanked him. He very tentatively moved his hand closer to hers on the grass and as their fingers touched, it was like an electric current running through both of them.

Maggie lifted her head and looked straight into his dark brown eyes, as she did, she felt this overwhelming sense of belonging, belonging to Alfonso in the purest sense of the word. He lent in toward her and ever so gently kissed her lips, which responded, as they never had before. It certainly wasn't the first time she had been kissed, but Maggie had never been kissed like this before and knew she never would again.

Maggie and Alfonso were oblivious to what the others were doing, they sat there holding hands and every now and then he would kiss her again. He had obviously been trying to learn a little English since they'd first met and they managed to talk about the important things.

Alfonso explained that he was from a village up in the mountains called, Barga, where he lived with his parents, older brother and younger sister. He was 18 years old, and was working in his uncle's ice-cream parlour over the summer, before he went to university. He wanted to be an architect and design the buildings of the future; he was so animated when he spoke, and although Maggie could not understand some of what he was saying, she understood enough to know that he would one day be an amazing architect.

Over the next few weeks, the girls went to 'Church' every Sunday and were able to find an excuse to spend one or two days in Lucca each week. Each time they met, the love Maggie and Alfonso had for each other grew stronger, but as the weeks passed, there was also this awful dark cloud of inevitability; the summer break was nearly over, and soon the girls would be heading home. Maggie honestly didn't know how she could go back home and leave him behind, although they promised faithfully that they would write to each other, and that they would find a way to meet up again.

On their last night together, Maggie and Alfonso had walked for ages, before sitting on the banks of the river. He presented her with the lovely coral and silver bracelet she'd seen the very first day she'd been in Lucca. She absolutely loved it and thanked him profusely for such a beautiful gift. It was a beautiful night, but there was no one else around. He kissed her gently at first but then their love for each other completely overwhelmed them and what happened next seemed like the most natural thing in the world.

Afterwards, Alfonso held Maggie tight not wanting to let go and he felt her tears as they flowed freely. "I will never forget you," she said. "I love you so much."

"I love you too, Mio Caro," he replied, "and we will see each other very soon. I will come to see you, lo prometto," he added—I promise.

Chapter 5

"And that's as much as I know, really," said Diane. "Your Mam came back from Italy and they wrote to each other every few days. Your grandparents became very suspicious of the letters arriving from Italy on a regular basis and intercepted one of them. They guessed what had happened and were horrified, they called your Mam a slut and a whore, and said they wanted nothing more to do with her."

Lianne was so upset by what Diane was telling her, she'd never met her grandparents, who had apparently died before she was born; how could they be so callous? It was clear that her Mam had loved Alfonso and it sounded as if he'd loved her too.

"It was only a few weeks later, that both your grandparents were killed in a car accident; your Mam was obviously distraught believing that she was somehow responsible, which obviously she wasn't. She was so overwhelmed by guilt and grief that she hadn't even noticed that she hadn't had a period since she'd got back from Italy, it was too late to do anything about the pregnancy—not that I think she would have anyway. But the one thing she decided, was not to tell Alfonso; it was her mistake and it seemed unfair to ruin the rest of his life with a baby they hadn't planned."

"Because your grandparents were gone, your Mam inherited the house and the savings they had had, so she decided she was luckier than most, and was going to go it alone. She stopped responding to Alfonso's letters; she couldn't bring herself to lie to him, so she decided it was best to say nothing at all. After a few months, Alfonso's letters stopped and the rest, as they say, is history. My Mam helped out, and I did what I could when you were born, as did your Mam's cousin Jennifer, on your grandmother's side. She never told any of us about Alfonso until several years later."

"But I don't understand? Why did she never tell me about Alfonso? I remember when I was very young, I mentioned a couple of times that all the other kids in school had Dads, why didn't I? She always fobbed me off with this story about how she and I were special, we were the dynamic duo and could do anything we wanted as long as we stuck together."

"I think she was probably ashamed," said Diane "and thought you'd think less of her somehow if you knew. You have to remember her parents were very strict, but even with them gone, the names they'd called her would have stayed with her, it would have eaten away at her. She made us all promise that we wouldn't say anything to you, she said she would tell you herself when the time was right. I suppose that time never came."

Lianne and Diane talked for a little longer. Then Lianne left clutching the wooden box that had opened up a whole other side of her Mam's life that she knew nothing about. Part of her felt angry about that, but then she tried to imagine what her Mam must have gone through. She'd lost her parents, the boy that she loved and she was pregnant; it must have been terrifying.

She arrived home and sat on the large comfy settee, curled up in a ball. Her mind was racing, suddenly she had a father who she knew nothing about really. She'd always assumed that her father was the result of a one-night stand, although in her heart she knew, her Mam wasn't that sort of person. As she'd grown up, she had stopped questioning her Mam about her father, but that hadn't stopped her imagining so many different scenarios.

He had been a famous film star who'd swept her Mam off her feet; a hero of some kind, who spent his days saving people's lives and then lost his own; a man from a wealthy family who had been forced by his parents to abandon her and marry some snotty nosed debutant, who had all the right connections. The truth was, that her father didn't even know that she existed, that he had truly loved her Mam and she had loved him so much that she'd never told him she was pregnant. It was a lot to take in.

Lianne lay on the settee all evening, staring at the wooden box until she eventually fell asleep. The following morning, she decided she needed to read through the letters and other bits that were in the box to try and make some sense of things.

She emptied the box on to the dining room table and tried to put things in date order—the photographs, the letters, etc. Her Mam looked so happy in the photos, she was older than Lianne had originally thought, but if her parents had been as strict as Diane had said, it wasn't surprising that her clothes and her hairstyle were more childish than the other girl, who appeared in a couple of the photos, who she now assumed was Jayne.

Lianne looked more closely now at the photos of Alfonso; it was the strangest sensation, this was her father, the man who had helped create her but who she had never known. He had a lovely smile and she could see why her Mam had fallen for him, she could also see where her dark hair and brown eyes had come from. She put the photos to one side and slowly undid the lilac ribbon that had been holding the letters together. She checked the postmark on each one to ensure she read them in the right order.

She hesitated as she picked up the first letter; should she be reading her Mam's personal letters? It felt like an intrusion of her Mam's privacy, but her Mam was no longer here and surely when she knew how ill she was, she would have got rid of them if she hadn't wanted Lianne to find them.

Margaret must have wanted Lianne to read them and know that she had been born because two young people had loved each other very much. Her father was no movie star, no hero, no son of a millionaire, but he was now very real and she no longer needed to imagine what he looked like.

She could now say that she looked like her dad, who was Italian.

Lianne carefully took the first letter out of the envelope and unfolded it. At the top was Alfonso's full name—Piacentini, Alfonso Piacentini. There was also an address in Barga, the village where Diane had said Alfonso was from. She started to read the words before her…

Mia Bella Maggie,

Only two days you go and I am missing you. You are most beautiful girl in the world and I am loving you so much. I so want to see you again.

I think maybe I not go to university in Italy, I go to UK instead so I can be with you.

I go to Barga tomorrow and talk to my father, so I come to see you and not go to university.

I am very happy I work in ice cream parlour this summer so I meet most beautiful person that I love. It seem Gino not planning to see Jayne, he now seeing other girl who live in Lucca.

**I not forget you Mia Bella Maggie. Con tango amore,
Alfonso xxx**

As she read through the other letters, one by one, she saw a clear pattern emerging. Alfonso's parents had obviously refused to allow him to give up his university place to travel to the UK after a girl, he'd only known for a few weeks. They had told him that if she really cared about him, she would wait and he could visit her the following summer, if he worked hard.

Alfonso was clearly distraught at the thought of not seeing Maggie and his next few letters talked of his undying love for her and that if she would just wait for him, they would be together in the end.

The tone of the next letter then changed, it was clear that she had told him that her parents had more or less disowned her, and his letter said that what had happened between them had happened out of love and she should not feel ashamed. After that, his next letter was obviously in response to the news that her parents had both died. He so wanted to be with her, to comfort her, to hold her, but respected her wish to be on her own for a while.

There were a couple more letters, in which again, he spoke of his undying love and that yes, if she could come to Italy now that her parents had gone, he would be the happiest man in the world. They could get a place near the university and he would get a job in the evenings to support her.

The final three or four letters were so hard for Lianne to read. Her mum had clearly stopped writing to Alfonso having found out that she was pregnant, and in his letters, he seemed so sad, so hurt. He could not understand why she was no longer writing to him, why she no longer loved him. Of course, Lianne knew it was the exact opposite, she had loved him so much that she felt she had to let him go and not tie him down with a child that neither of them had planned.

By the time Lianne had finished reading through all the letters, she felt emotionally drained. As she made herself another coffee, her phone pinged; it was a text from Gemma, one of her oldest and dearest friends. She asked if Lianne fancied meeting up for a drink that evening, and how she thought it would do Lianne good to get out for a few hours. It was the last thing that Lianne felt like doing, but she found herself agreeing to a quiet drink and made arrangements before heading upstairs to shower.

The last time Lianne had seen Gemma, was at her mum's funeral; they had texted each other every day, but Gemma had no idea what had happened over the last few days, it had taken Lianne long enough to come to terms with what she had found and then heard from Diane. It wasn't the sort of thing you just dropped into a text 'Oh and by the way I've found out my dad's Italian!'

They met in one of Lianne's locals and when she arrived, Gemma was already sitting at a table with two glasses of wine in front of her. "I hope one of those is for me," Lianne said, hoping to sound quite light—hearted about things.

"Of course," came the reply "unless I get a better offer!"

Gemma stood up and the two friends hugged for what seemed like an eternity "Now, I know something is up," Gemma said. "You were hanging on to me pretty tightly there Mrs, spill the beans!" Gemma immediately regretted what she'd said, "I'm so sorry, that was a stupid thing to say! After everything you've been through in the last few weeks, I'm surprised you're still functioning. I don't think I would be in the circumstances. I have to say Li, you're looking like shite, you've lost weight and you don't look as if you're getting much sleep."

Lianne smiled, she could always rely on Gemma to be completely honest, even blunt sometimes; it was one of the things she loved about her, there was no side to Gemma. She would never talk about you behind your back, she was far more likely to tell you to your face that you looked like crap!

"Let me get us another drink," Lianne said, "and then I'll tell you everything." She returned from the bar a few moments later with a bottle of wine rather than two glasses, and poured her heart out.

She told Gemma all about the box she'd found, what Diane had told her, and then what she'd read in Alfonso's letters.

Chapter 6

"Bloody hell Li, I did not expect that. You never spoke about your dad, so I just assumed he'd done a runner when you were young. Shit! This is huge, not only is your father probably still alive, he has no idea you even exist! You could have half brothers and sisters in Italy! Wow cheap holidays! Sorry, I was being insensitive again."

Lianne laughed, a genuine laugh this time, probably the first since her mum had gone. "I knew I could rely on you to see the positive side to all this," she said, squeezing Gemma's hand. "The question now, I suppose, is what do I do with the information that I've got it? I can't imagine Alfonso would be very happy if I just turned up and said, 'Hi you don't know me, but I'm your long-lost daughter'."

"That probably is a little too blunt, even for me, but come off it Li, you can't walk away and pretend you never found the box. It'll eat away at you."

"So, what do I do? There could be hundreds of Alfonso Piacentini's in Italy, I wouldn't know where to start."

"But that's not strictly true, is it? You have the guy's name, the address of where he was living, albeit 30 years ago, and you know he was training to be an architect. That's got to narrow the field down, surely? And you can find anyone these days on Google! Have you searched for him?"

"No," Lianne said, "to be honest I didn't even think of it. So, what if I Google him and find him, then what do I do?"

"It's simple," Gemma replied, "you go and see him. He obviously loved your mum a great deal and she loved him so much, she was prepared to let him go. You have to tell him the truth Li, I think it's what your mum would have wanted, otherwise she would have destroyed the letters, photos, everything, a long time ago."

"Do you really think so? What if he doesn't want anything to do with me? Then what?"

"I really do think so. And if he doesn't want anything to do with you, then he's not the man your mum thought he was, and at least you'll know you've tried. If you're going to do this, you need to do it now whilst you still have the opportunity to have a relationship with him, if that's what you want. There's no point in waiting until you're old and grey; it'll be too late by then. And if it doesn't work out, then that's that, but at least you will have tried."

The girls chatted for another half hour and then Gemma said she'd have to head off, as she had to be up early in the morning for work. "I'll ring you tomorrow evening," she said, "and you can tell me what you've found." With that, the girls hugged again and then both set off home.

Lianne resisted the temptation to get her iPad out and start the search, it was already 10:00 p.m. and she was exhausted. She was also feeling hungry, something she hadn't felt for a long time, so she made herself a cup of tea and a piece of toast and turned the TV on for a while, before she headed to bed.

Lianne slept well, despite everything, and woke feeling a lot calmer about things. She knew what she was going to do and that helped to dissipate the anxiety she had been feeling since she found the box.

She headed down to the kitchen and switched on the kettle, she couldn't do anything until she'd had her first cuppa in the morning. "Just like you Mum," she said out loud and smiled to herself. They had been so similar in many respects and the fact that neither could function without a cup of tea in the morning was just one of those similarities.

She drank her tea and then decided to make another, before she opened up her laptop. She let out a deep sigh as the screen came to life and then opened her browser "Ok then Google, let's see what you've got." She typed the words 'Alfonso Piacentini Architect' and pressed the search button; she was amazed as to how many results suddenly appeared before her. But when she looked more carefully, only the first half a dozen or so were of any interest.

She opened each link one at a time and dismissed the first two, they were certainly not the Alfonso Piacentini that she was looking for—the one was far too old and the other was an Australian. The third one looked a little more promising, and with the help of Google translate, she managed to confirm that he was about the right age and that he had done some work in Tuscany. Which was the area she knew Barga and Lucca were in. There was a small photograph and when she compared it to the one, she had of Alfonso, taken 30 years ago, there was certainly a similarity.

Lianne decided to look for Alfonso in Barga or Lucca, and it quickly became apparent that Piacentini was a common surname like 'Smith' or 'Williams', so that proved fruitless, as there were dozens of A Piacentini's. She went back to the original article she had first found and translated a bit more. There was nothing to say where this Alfonso lived or worked, so no way really of contacting him. Mind you, she had absolutely no idea what she would say anyway! She couldn't just send an email or letter that said 'Hi, I think you're my dad!' could she? The poor guy could end up having a heart attack.

She wrote down everything she had found and then closed the laptop. Now, she decided, she needed to get out and get some air; it was cold outside, but the sky was clear blue. She got herself dressed and grabbed her coat, hat and gloves. She put her phone in her pocket and grabbed her car keys.

Lianne headed for Caerphilly Mountain, which at this time of day, was only a 20-minute drive. She parked the car and wrapped herself up, before heading up to the top. There were a handful of hardy dog walkers on the mountain, braving the easterly wind that was making itself felt on the mountain side. She saw one little Yorkshire Terrier who looked as if he would be blown away by the next gust of wind; and then there was a stupid Springer Spaniel bounding through the undergrowth, he seemed to be on springs and his ears were flapping as he surfaced above the ferns and brambles with every bounce. Lianne couldn't help but smile.

She carried on walking up to the top and found a ledge to sit on, as she looked out over Caerphilly itself. She could see the bustling town below her and the medieval castle which had its own leaning tower. Lianne sat there for about 10 minutes reminiscing, her mum would often take her up the mountain when she was a child, and they would stop for ice-cream on the way home. Far too cold for ice-cream today, but maybe a nice hot chocolate in the Mountain Cafe by the car park.

As Lianne started to head down to the café, she wondered if Caerphilly's leaning tower reminded her mum of Italy and that's why she loved the mountain so much. Not that her mum had ever been to Pisa as far as she was aware, but everything had a link to Italy, even the ice-cream, or was she allowing her imagination to take over?

As she sat enjoying her hot chocolate—with extra marshmallows—she thought again of what she'd found on the internet; it wasn't very much at all and certainly not enough to send an email or a letter to a man who may or may not be her dad.

She told Gemma as much when she phoned that evening. "I really don't think there's any more I can do," she said, "I just don't have enough to go on."

"Not enough to write I agree, but I think you're missing something here," Gemma replied. "You need to get your backside on a flight to Italy!" She added as if it was the most natural thing in the world.

"Don't you think that's a bit OTT! I wouldn't know where to start looking."

"OK, how's this for an idea, why don't you and I go, and spend a long weekend in Italy? I've got time owing to me and you're not due back in work for another few weeks; let's just go and spend some time where your mum and dad met, and fell in love. See the places they went to, retrace their steps. What do you think?"

"Well, it's not completely crazy," Lianne replied, "we could hire a car, find somewhere to stay…are you sure you don't mind coming with me? I wouldn't want to go on my own."

"Don't be daft! I'd love to come with you. Now how about you check out flights, etc, tomorrow, and then I'll call in on my way home from work and we can take it from there!"

"Perfect," Lianne said. "I'll cook!"

"I was hoping you'd say that," Gemma laughed, "now go and get some sleep!"

Lianne headed up to bed a short time later; as she climbed into bed and snuggled under the duvet, her mind was already beginning to wander. Did she honestly think she could just arrive in Italy and that her father would magically appear? It was a crazy idea, wasn't it? She must be bonkers but as Gemma said, she had nothing to lose.

Once again, by the time the morning came, Lianne felt as if she hadn't had any sleep, her mind was going round and round in circles and she had failed to make any decision as to whether she should travel to Italy or not. Lianne was a very sensible person. She never did anything without thinking it through carefully; maybe a little too much sometimes. As she climbed out of bed and stepped into the shower, she could almost hear her mum saying, "It's about time you went and had some fun Lianne." Her mum always use to try and encourage her to take a day off from her studies now and again and to live a little.

To most parents, Lianne probably seemed like the perfect child, always did her homework on time, her head always in a book as she studied for her degree. But Margaret always felt that there was something almost unhealthy about Lianne's diligence and she would encourage her to take time out and do all the things a normal teenager did. In hindsight, Lianne wondered if this was her Mam wanting to relive her youth through her.

Gemma arrived at the house at about 6:30 p.m. There was a lasagne in the oven and she thought Lianne looked better than she had in weeks.

"So," Gemma said as Lianne handed her a glass of wine, "what did you find out?"

"Well, we can get a flight from Bristol to Pisa, and either get a train, or hire a car to take us to Lucca," Lianne replied, "and I took a look on Airbnb, and we can get an apartment for a few days or a hotel, whichever we prefer."

"Bloody hell," Gemma said. "I was waiting for the list of all the reasons you'd thought of as to why we shouldn't go! I've already compiled a list of reasons I was going to give you as to why we should! OMG I'm amazed!"

"Well," Lianne replied, "I realised that if I don't do it now, I never will. Finding my dad is probably impossible, but it would be nice to know where I came from. Just to see places I know my mum saw, places she fell in love with and the places she was when she fell in love. Do you think I'm bonkers?"

"Not at all, I think it's a lovely idea, you know so little about your mum before she had you, you could almost retrace her footsteps."

"That's what I thought; maybe it would help me now, that Mam's not here, if I knew who she was before I came along. She must have been terrified, knowing she was pregnant and losing her parents at the same time; she obviously had an inner strength, even then."

By the time Gemma left Lianne's, later that evening, the flights were booked and they'd rented a 2-bedroom apartment, just 5 minutes' walk from Lucca's historic town centre. Lianne felt strangely calm, almost as if it was meant to be, and that night she dreamt of her Mam, a dream so vivid, that it was as if her Mam was there with her. She cried softly when she woke and realised that she was alone, but somehow, she felt as if she wasn't—not really.

Later that day, Lianne popped over to see Diane again and she told her what she'd decided to do.

"I know it's crazy and that the chances of finding my dad are a billion to one, but from everything that was in that box, it's clear that Mam really loved him and I think he loved her too. So, I want to see where they met and fell in love, do you think I'm mad? I probably am, travelling all that way on a whim."

"I don't think you're mad Lianne, I think it sounds perfect, and if nothing else, you'll have a break before you have to go back to work. It'll be a holiday for you and I think you need that, after the last couple of years."

They chatted for another hour or so, about Margaret, and the hand that fate had dealt her. It was so sad to have loved and lost so long ago, but Diane reminded Lianne that Margaret had been incredibly proud of her and that she wouldn't have changed a thing. Lianne promised to take lots of photos and left, saying she would call over when she got back.

Chapter 7

Three days later the girls were at Bristol airport, waiting for their early morning flight to Pisa. Both only had hand luggage, and Lianne had carefully packed a few photos and things from her Mam's box which she thought would help them get their bearings.

The flight was on time, and they landed in Italy to some glorious spring weather; they quickly found their private transfer and within an hour of landing, they were heading the short distance to Lucca.

They found their way to the apartment, and were greeted by an elderly lady who showed them around, and gave them a key. She had left a small supply of groceries, and both girls realised how hungry they were, having eaten very little all day. So they tucked into the cheese, meats and salad with some delicious fresh bread, which they followed with some fresh fruit and a glass of wine.

The top floor apartment had a small balcony and the girls sat outside in the sun, as they sipped their wine. Both were tired from the early start they had had, but both felt strangely exhilarated that they were actually in Lucca.

"How do you feel Lianne?" Gemma asked, "it must feel really strange to be here."

"I won't lie, I feel completely overwhelmed at the moment," Lianne replied, "to think that if Mam hadn't come here all those years ago, I wouldn't exist. That must sound daft, but I have the strangest feeling of being 'home'; of being where I'm supposed to be."

"I don't think you're daft at all, not at all."

Gemma poured them another glass of wine each, and they sat in silence on balcony enjoying the Spring sunshine. A short while later they unpacked their bags and then decided to take a walk. They had no plan, no destination in mind, they just wanted to soak up some of the atmosphere and enjoy the sunshine. They needed provisions and so, would look for *la drogheria*—a grocers—where they could pick up a few bits and pieces, and maybe find somewhere they could eat that evening.

By the time they returned to the apartment, they were both shattered and decided to try the small pizzeria they had found, literally around the corner, before having an early night.

The next day, both girls woke early as the sunshine streamed through the thin organza curtains, they had breakfast and then formulated their plan for the day. Lianne had obtained a map of the town and had managed to plot out the key buildings that her Mam had photos of, so they had some idea of where they were heading. She was under no illusions about finding her father, it was going to be more or less impossible but at least she could see some of the places her parents had gone to.

Lianne had no idea where the ice-cream parlour was, but she was able to find the church where her parents had met that first Sunday, and she thought she had worked out where the park was, that they had walked to. Obviously, the river was where it always was, but she had no way of knowing exactly where on the river her parents had been. But they had come up with a plan and having plastered on some sunscreen, they were ready to leave.

"Don't you have some more sensible shoes?" Lianne asked. "Those are beautiful, but I don't know if they're the best thing to be wearing, we're going to be doing a lot of walking."

Gemma assured her that she would be absolutely fine and they headed off. Lianne smiled to herself, her and Gemma were so different, not only in their physical appearance—Gemma was a striking blonde—but also the way they dressed. Both wore shorts, but whilst Lianne had a t-shirt and proper walking shoes, Gemma had a skimpy vest top and was wearing some strappy gold sandals. *Totally inappropriate attire for sightseeing, but typical of Gemma*, Lianne thought!

Lucca was a beautiful place and the girls walked for a couple of hours, before stopping in the Piazza dell' Anfiteatro, for a cold drink under the shade of one of the cafe umbrellas. Gemma slipped off her sandals and rubbed her feet, Lianne smiled at her. "Everything OK?" She asked.

"Absolutely fine," came the reply, and Lianne laughed.

They finished their drinks and decided to head off down one of the many small streets that seemed to be full of shops of every kind, from high class boutiques, to souvenir shops, and numerous cafes that filled the air with the delicious scent of coffee, fresh bread, and numerous other enticing aromas.

They had only been walking for about 10 minutes, when Gemma yelled out "Shit!" and Lianne turned to see that Gemma had lost her footing and gone over on her ankle. She carefully helped her friend to a nearby chair and took off her gold sandal.

"Don't say it," Gemma said before Lianne could even open her mouth, "You were right, these sandals weren't the best idea I've ever had! But you have to admit they are absolutely gorgeous, aren't they?" Lianne couldn't help but laugh and soon Gemma was laughing too. "OK, no more silly sandals for me!"

Suddenly they were both conscious of a well-dressed young man standing next to them.

"Scusami, posso aiutarti?" He asked. Neither Lianne or Gemma had a clue what this guy had said to them, but the look on their faces was enough for him to realise that they weren't Italian.

"May I help you?" He asked. "You are hurt?"

"My ankle," Gemma replied, feeling very grateful that she had shaved her legs and put on some fake tan.

"May I?" He asked, kneeling at her feet.

She nodded and with that, he gently examined her ankle. Both girls couldn't help but stare at him, he was tall and incredibly handsome in light brown chinos, with a white polo shirt that accentuated his dark brown hair and tanned skin.

"It is just…um…sprained, I think you say." With that, he stood up and saw the expression on both girls faces, thinking he'd done something wrong he quickly apologised. "Perdonami…um…excuse me, I am doctor—not just touch lady's ankle!" The girls both laughed, and he smiled at them.

"I am Gemma," the patient said, "and this is Lianne. Thank you for your help."

"You most welcome," came the reply "can I get anything for you?"

"No thank you," Lianne said, "we'll rest awhile and then head back. Thank you again." With that the man left, and the girls looked at each other and laughed.

"No wonder your Mam fell for an Italian," Gemma said, "he was gorgeous! Did you see those eyes? I could have lost myself in his eyes! He was amazing and so gentle, he…"

Gemma was suddenly aware that Lianne wasn't listening, she was staring up at the shop which Gemma had been sat outside.

It was an ice cream parlour, "Titolare: G. Piacentini."

Chapter 8

Lianne didn't say a word, and Gemma had no idea what had just happened, but she decided that they needed to go back to the apartment. Somehow, Gemma managed to hobble to a main road where she flagged down a taxi and the girls made their way back to the apartment, barely saying a word. Gemma was quite worried, her friend looked pale despite her olive complexion, and just seemed to be staring out of the taxi window.

When they got back to the apartment, Gemma made Lianne sit down and she then opened a bottle of wine and gave her friend a glass.

"OK," she said, "I don't really know what happened back there, but something freaked you out, and it's scared the hell out of me!"

It was a few moments before Lianne spoke, "I think I told you that my parents met at an ice-cream parlour." Gemma nodded. "I know there must be hundreds of ice-cream parlours in Lucca, but the one where my parents met belonged to Alfonso's uncle. I never thought about it before, but there's a 50% chance that Alfonso's cousin was on his dad's side of the family, so he may very well have been a Piacentini too and his cousin would have been Gino Piacentini. It was a family business, so Gino may have taken it on over in time, after all, he must be in his late 40s early 50s like my dad…Do you see where I'm going with this?"

"OMG! So, you think where we were today, may have been 'the' actual place where your folks met. Bloody hell, that's heavy stuff. And to think, if I hadn't worn those stupid sandals, I wouldn't have twisted my ankle outside the shop!"

"Of course, maybe I am completely wrong," Lianne said, "but it was such a shock to see the name written there."

"OK, well, we need to decide what we're going to do next; we need a plan. But I think first we both need to rest and then we need to eat—I'm starving as always! Why don't we take it easy for an hour, then we can shower and change. We passed a nice-looking trattoria not far from here, so we can get something to eat there if you like, and have a proper chat about where we go from here. What do you say?"

"This is crazy Gemma, I never expected to actually find the place! But you're right, we need to eat, can you walk to the restaurant?"

Gemma said she'd be fine; she'd seen a first aid kit in one of the kitchen drawers so would strap her ankle up, and wear sensible—if boring—flat shoes. Lianne laughed and with that, both girls went to their rooms to lie down for an hour, before getting ready.

They left the apartment a little while later, and walked slowly to the restaurant. It was a beautiful evening, the sky was clear and it promised to be another glorious day tomorrow. The air was filled with spicy aromas as they approached the restaurant and were shown to a table outside, where they could watch the world go by. Both ordered pasta and it was only when they had eaten that and several slices of focaccia, did the conversation turn to the events of the afternoon.

"The ball is entirely in your court Li," Gemma said, "I'm not going to force you to do anything. We can go back to the shop and see if it is the same one, or you can forget all about it and we'll just carry on doing the tourist bit. It's up to you."

"I don't think I can just walk away. Really, can I? We came to Lucca to see if I could find out anything about my dad, I'd be stupid to run away just because I might have found something. I have to at least ask if it's Gino's shop, don't you think? Otherwise, I'll never forgive myself, and we've come this far."

Gemma agreed and as the waiter came to take their order for dessert, the girls decided that provided Lianne felt the same in the morning, they would head back into Lucca to see what they could find out.

"I need the loo," Lianne said, and as she stood up and walked into the restaurant, she managed to bump into a guy coming out.

"I'm so sorry," she said, looking up into the eyes of the doctor who had helped Gemma earlier. He smiled at her with a smile that lit up the room, and created a feeling in a part of Lianne's heart that she thought at died a long time ago.

"How is the patient?" He asked, "not wearing gold sandals I hope!"

"She's fine," Lianne said, "we just came out to get something to eat. I must thank you for looking after Gemma earlier, you were most kind, and I didn't get to thank you."

"Not necessary," he said, "but you may buy me a drink if you wish!"

Lianne was a bit taken aback, but agreed. "I am Lianne by the way," she said.

"Ricardo Moretti, Doctor Ricardo Moretti."

"Pleased to meet you, Doctor Moretti. Gemma and I are sitting out front if you'd care to join us."

"Ricardo please, and si, I would like to sit with you."

Lianne went on into the bathroom and when she returned to the table, she found Ricardo sitting at the table with Gemma. Her jaw had literally fallen to the floor, as she'd spotted the dashing doctor. By the time Lianne had joined them, Gemma already had her leg on the doctor's lap asking him if he would re bandage it, as she was "sure she'd made a mess of it." Lianne laughed as she sat down, *typical of Gemma* she thought. She ordered more wine and the three chatted about Gemma's choice of footwear, as well as the girl's complete disinterest in football!

"We're Welsh you see," Gemma said, "we're more into rugby than football."

"Ah yes, six nations rugby," Ricardo said, "my friend, he play rugby for team here. Get very dirty!" The girls laughed; Ricardo didn't look like the sort of guy to get muddy!

Eventually Ricardo asked what the girls were doing in Lucca. Gemma looked at Lianne as if to say, 'it's up to you whether you want to tell him or not.' Lianne didn't say anything and so Gemma said they'd just decided to have a long weekend away, and had got last minute flights, when Lianne blurted out "I've come to find my father."

Ricardo looked completely stunned, as if he'd misheard what Lianne had said. With that, Lianne told Ricardo an abbreviated version of how she'd found out that her father was from the area and she'd come to retrace her mother's footsteps. By the time she'd finished, Ricardo seemed genuinely concerned for her.

"What if you find him?" He asked, "he may not want to see you, he have wife and children maybe."

"I realise that, he may not even remember my Mam, but I want to at least try if only to let him know that Mam always loved him. There was never anyone else."

All three were silent, as if lost in their own thoughts, and the significance of what had been said hung in the air. It was Gemma who broke the silence a few minutes later by bringing the conversation around to more light hearted topics, and asking about Ricardo's rugby mate.

"Ah si, Marco. He play tomorrow, you come see?"

"Definitely," said Gemma with a wicked grin across her face. "I like men in shorts!"

Gemma and Lianne both laughed. It was typical of Gemma to bring the subject back to men, Lianne thought. It was one of the many reasons Lianne loved her, she was the sister she'd never had, and one of the few people Lianne could be completely honest with, even if she was obsessed with the opposite sex!

"I'm not sure," Lianne said honestly, "we were going to go back to the ice-cream parlour to see if it is actually the one where my dad worked."

"I understand," Ricardo responded. "But if you come watch the rugby tomorrow, I help you after to find your father."

Gemma's eyes were pleading with Lianne "OK," she said, "it's a deal!"

Ricardo left the girls at that point, and arranged to pick them up the following morning. "Fino a domani signore—until tomorrow," he said.

When they returned to the apartment, Lianne was very quiet; Gemma took a bottle of wine from the fridge and ushered Li on to the balcony. She lit a few citronella candles, designed to keep the mosquitoes away, and both sat in silence. Despite Gemma's sometimes brash appearance and her love of men, she was also a very sensitive person, and knew better than to force Li to open up; she'd say something when she was ready.

A few moments later, they heard church bells in the distance and Li quietly said, "What if I do find him and he wants nothing to do with me? What if he doesn't even remember my Mam? What if…"

"Stop right there, Li. Your Mam was a beautiful person, inside and out. She was not the sort of person to fall for some Italian lothario, that's the sort of thing I'd do! And anyway, from all the letters you have, etc you know your Mam meant the world to him, so you can stop the 'what ifs'. If we find him, we'll take it from there, and at the end of the day, whatever happens, you'll be no worse off than you are now. OK?"

Lianne smiled, "You're right, I know you're right. It just got to me hearing Ricardo say it out loud."

"Well, I think you got to Ricardo, he couldn't keep his eyes off you Li! Your very own Italian stallion and a doctor to boot!" Both girls laughed and with that, they started reminiscing about some of the ridiculous things they had got up to over the years.

The girls finished the bottle of wine and talked a little longer. They agreed that they'd go to meet Ricardo's friends in the morning and would head back to the ice-cream parlour in the afternoon. It was Saturday tomorrow and they didn't want to leave it until the Sunday, in case it was closed, and then on Monday they were due to fly home.

With that, the girls hugged one another and said goodnight.

"Love you."

"Love you too."

Chapter 9

Again, the girls woke to the sun streaming through the flimsy curtains, both slept well, and Li found Gemma already in the kitchen, when she got up. The room was filled with the smell of coffee and fresh pastries.

"I popped to the little bakery around the corner," she said, "thought we could do with something a bit more substantial today." She poured Li a coffee, and offered her a plate of delicious pastries.

"Where to start!" She said, but only hesitated for a moment before diving in. 2 coffees and 3 pastries later, both of them felt completely stuffed. "I could never live here," Li said. "I'd be the size of a house in no time!"

Gemma laughed, "Me too!"

They sat on the balcony looking out over the city for half an hour or so. They didn't really talk—there was no need to, they were so close that they never felt the need to fill the empty silences. Then it was time to get ready before Ricardo arrived, he'd said he would pick them up at 10:30 a.m. The game would have started by the time they got there, but he didn't think the girls would want to sit through a full game.

He was wearing a pair of navy shorts, when he arrived, with a salmon pink t-shirt. Li spotted the designer label, and reckoned it probably cost him more than her entire outfit. But whatever it cost, there was no doubting that he was a really good-looking guy, and Li felt her stomach churning as he took her hand and helped her into the car.

"I see you have good shoes today, Gemma," he said and they all laughed.

And with that, he started the engine and they headed out of the city toward Capannori. It was another beautiful day and he had the roof down on the car. It didn't take them long to get to the rugby ground, and several people smiled at Ricardo and spoke to him, as he showed the girls to some seats.

"More patients?" Gemma asked.

"No," came the reply "I used to play, that how I know Marco, but…um… how you say?" And with that, he pointed to a thin white scar on his knee, "Legamento?"

"Ah, ligament damage."

"Si."

Ricardo tried several times to point out Marco to them, but all the players were moving so fast it was impossible to work out which one he was, so Ricardo gave up trying. He focussed more on the game and Li worked out he was supporting the team in green, and that he was probably swearing in Italian on occasions!

It was fun to watch the game and to watch Ricardo. He seemed like a really nice guy, but Li wasn't looking for some brief holiday romance; Gemma on the other hand, was in her element watching numerous hunky Italians running up and down the pitch in skimpy shorts!

The game ended—the green team won—and one of the players spotted Ricardo and came over. "Ciao amico, chi è il dottore bello oggi?"

"Buono, buono. Marco, meet Gemma and Lianne. They come from Wales to see proper rugby!"

With that, they all laughed. Marco greeted both girls warmly and said Ricardo had not told him how beautiful the women were that were coming to see him play. Both girls blushed; Marco was obviously a charmer, but he was also very handsome in a rugged way. A little shorter than Ricardo, with the characteristic dark-hair and olive skin, he had obviously broken his nose a few times, but all Gemma saw was his broad chest and bulging biceps.

"For goodness's sake," Lianne said in a whisper to Gemma, "pull yourself together woman, you're practically drooling!" Both women laughed, and with that Marco suggested that Ricardo take the girls to a nearby bar whilst he showered and changed. Gemma's face broke in broad grin and Lianne, nudged in a playful manner, knowing exactly what her friend was thinking!

"Come ladies," Ricardo said, leading them back to the car, and then added, "Marco meet us when dressed." With that, both girls dissolved into the giggles, and poor Ricardo had no idea what was so funny.

Ricardo drove the girls to the Cafe Arianna, which was just a few minutes down the road. Like many such places in Italy, it was very much a family business that catered for families. It served food and alcohol, but both women opted for a coffee, given that it wasn't even lunchtime. Ricardo ordered a soft drink for himself and a beer for Marco, who joined them about 15 minutes later. The drinks arrived with a plate of small but delicious biscuits, which they devoured, as they chatted about various things. Marco ordered some more drinks, refusing to allow the girls to pay, and the conversation turned to Lianne and her quest to find Alfonso.

"So, seignorina, Ricardo tell me you looking for Italian family." It was clear Ricardo had not told Marco the whole story, and Lianne appreciated his discretion, but saw no reason to lie.

"My father," she replied, and saw the look of amazement on Marco's face. With that, she told Marco briefly how her parents had met, but that her father knew nothing about her. As she finished, all four sat in relative silence, as Marco pondered on what he had been told.

He nodded his head a few times and said, "This is why you very beautiful!" Lianne looked completely baffled, and Marco said something to Ricardo in Italian.

"What Marco say," Ricardo said, "is you very beautiful because you are half Italian!" With that both girls understood Marco's jokey comment and smiled.

"Gracie," Lianne replied.

Lianne went on to explain the possible significance of the ice-cream parlour where they had met Ricardo the previous day, and her intention to go back there that afternoon to see if there really was a connection between the shop's owner and Lianne's father. With that, Ricardo reiterated his offer to go with the girls, saying that it may make things easier if he was there to explain things in Italian. Lianne and Gemma looked at each other and both agreed it would make a lot of sense to have Ricardo there.

They finished their drinks, and Ricardo said he would drive the girls back to Lucca; Marco explained that he had work that afternoon, but suggested that they all meet the following evening for a bite to eat, before the girls headed back home.

Arrangements made, the girls said goodbye to Marco and got into Ricardo's car, for the short journey back to Lucca.

Chapter 10

Once they reached Lucca, Ricardo guided the girls through the streets to the street on which he'd met them the day before. The ice-,cream parlour was busy and so they waited awhile before going inside. Ricardo asked to speak to the owner and Lianne was very disappointed when a young man in his early twenties came forward to speak to them. He spoke to Ricardo for a few minutes and Ricardo gave him what appeared to be a business card.

With that, Ricardo led the girls back outside, and Lianne felt an overwhelming sense of disappointment. She wasn't sure what she'd expected, but she had hoped and prayed that there was a connection between her father and the ice-cream parlour. But there was no way the young man they had met was her father's cousin. It was a massive anti-climax.

Ricardo said nothing as they left the shop and guided them through the narrow streets to a small cafe, where he ordered them all drinks.

"Well?" Gemma said. "What was that all about?"

Ricardo explained that the young man was indeed called Gino Piacentini and he had been named after his father who had died before he was born. He had inherited the ice-cream parlour from his grandfather, but had had little to do with him. Consequently, he had no idea if his father had had a cousin called Alfonso, but he would see what he could find out. Ricardo had given the man his card, so that he could contact him if he found out anything.

"Oh." was all Lianne could bring herself to say. "That's it then, there's nothing more we can do."

Neither Ricardo or Gemma had anything to say, other than to agree with her. They all made their way back to the car and Ricardo dropped the girls off at their apartment, saying that he and Marco would pick them up at 7:30 p.m. the following evening. Both Lianne and Gemma thanked him for all his help, and said goodbye before making their way into the apartment.

It was clear that Lianne was disappointed, and Gemma felt certain that her friend had probably had unrealistic expectations. She said little, but opened a bottle of wine and followed Lianne on to the balcony with 2 glasses.

Lianne didn't say anything for a very long time, she sat quietly looking out over the city and slowly sipping her wine.

"I think I'd like to see Barga before we leave, I want to hire a car first thing tomorrow and take a drive up there," she said, before adding. "You don't have to come with me, if you don't want to."

"Of course, I'll come with you, don't be so daft. We're in this together." With that, Gemma got up and checked the few provisions they had, before saying, "An omelette and salad for tea, won't take me long."

After they had eaten, Lianne headed for her room whilst Gemma checked out car rental places and maps. As Lianne lay on the bed, she found herself talking to her mum and then the tears slowly started rolling down her cheeks.

"This was a stupid idea Mam, what on Earth possessed me to come all this way to find a man I've never met! Did I honestly think I could just turn up at the ice-cream parlour, and Gino and Alfonso would suddenly appear? I must be bloody mad! I'm sorry Mam, sorry for everything; if it hadn't been for me, maybe you and Alfonso would have been able to make a go of things."

She could almost hear her Mam shouting at her, "Stop it! Stop it! Stop it! That's a ridiculous thing to say." *Oh, Mam. I miss you so much*, Lianne thought, *what on earth am I going to do without you?* With that, the tears flowed more freely and she sobbed quietly for 20 minutes or so, before falling into a deep sleep.

Chapter 11

Lianne woke at about 7.30 the next morning, and she could hear the church bells ringing in the distance. She was surprised to see that Gemma was already up and dressed.

"Morning sleepyhead!" Gemma said with a smile. "Ok the car hire place opens at 9:00 a.m. and I've already pre-booked a car for the day. The place is about 10 minutes' walk from here, so you have plenty of time to shower and have some breakfast. You go jump in the shower, and I'll make another pot of coffee."

"Ok. Yes sir!" came the reply, then, "Gem I'm really sorry about…" Before she could finish, Gemma told her that no apology was necessary, it had been an emotional few days, and as Lianne's best-friend, Gemma said it was her duty to be there for her through good times and bad.

"Now get your arse in that shower, pronto young lady, or else!"

By 8:45 a.m. both of them were ready. They both wore shorts and t-shirts, along with sensible shoes, even Gemma had managed to find some relatively flat shoes to wear. They also grabbed some sweaters, as they knew it could be colder in the mountains.

It took about an hour to get to Barga, the road was winding and narrow in parts, so they took their time and chatted, as they headed up into the hills. When they finally arrived, it seemed that the village was in two halves that straddled a narrow gorge, and on the bridge that joined the two halves there was a red, British phone box, which looked totally out of place.

There were also a number of Scottish flags flying, which seemed very odd. They found somewhere to park and headed to a nearby café, on a small-town square. They ordered a coffee, and they used Google maps to work out exactly where they were. They were also able to establish that there was a tourist information office on the other side of the bridge, and so decided to head there.

As they crossed the bridge, they could see that the town comprised of two distinct areas, the newer area, where they had had their coffee and a much older area with cobbled walkways that led up to the top of the hill. They found the tourist office quite quickly and were able to get a proper map. They also picked up a number of leaflets, and in one of those, Gemma read that Barga was known as 'the most Scottish town in Italy'.

Apparently, it was something to do with the large number of Italians who had left Barga in the late 19th Century, looking for work, and ended up in Scotland. Barga also boasted its own 'fish and chip' festival later in the year, which seemed decidedly odd, but it made the town even more intriguing.

The girls studied the map, they had no particular place to go and so decided to wend their way through the cobbled streets and up the hill, to what appeared to be a large church at the top.

The view from the top, when they got there, was incredible. You could see across the rooftops of Barga to the hills beyond, and as they had thought, there was a large stone church with a central tower at the front.

"Wow!" Gemma said, "this place is incredible! Look at the view over there! Amazing!"

"It certainly is spectacular," Lianne replied. "It's crazy to think my dad was living here somewhere, that I may have brothers or sisters, grandparents, all within a stone's throw. Strange. My dad probably went to this church with his family when he was a child, it's bonkers."

Lianne walked up the steps on the right-hand side of the church to admire the view from a different angle, and then said she wanted to take a look inside the church.

You could feel the cooler air as soon as you walked inside the church, there were no seats in the church, just a big open space with two large stone lions which were cordoned off. Down, each side of the church, were a series of archways that stood on high columns stretching up to the vaulted wooden ceiling. It was very peaceful and Lianne felt strangely calm, as she walked down toward the altar. She then noticed a smaller altar to the side, where you could light candles and she headed toward it.

She lit a candle in memory of her Mam, and then a second, "This is for you Dad, wherever you are and whoever you are." Lianne then knelt down and prayed quietly for a few moments, before heading out of the church. As she did so, she saw table with a visitors book; numerous people had written entries commenting on the beautiful church and referring to family that had lived in the area. Lianne thought for a moment and then picked up a pen.

Barga is a beautiful place and it is a part of me now. I want Alfonso to know that Maggie never stopped loving him and I am proof of that.

Lianne walked back out into the bright sunshine, and found Gemma sitting on the steps. "You, OK?" Gemma asked.

"I will be," came the reply.

The girls decided to get a bite to eat before heading back to Lucca, and headed back towards the cafe where they had had coffee earlier. They each ordered a slice of pizza and a soft drink, and then went and sat on a table outside in the sunshine.

"Are you glad you came?" Gemma asked.

"Definitely, it's certainly a beautiful place. And even if I never find my father, at least I know where he lived and I can picture him in my mind praying in the church or even sitting in this cafe."

"Do you want to try and find the address that was on the letters he sent to your Mam?"

"No, I don't think so, what would it achieve? I can 'imagine' him growing up in Barga, seeing the house wouldn't make any difference, and all the houses look so similar anyway, so it wouldn't mean anything."

"I can see that," Gemma said, "you wouldn't be able to see anything other than the facade of the building, and as you say they all look pretty similar."

"Exactly, so I think we have our lunch and then head back to Lucca."

The girls arrived back in Lucca just after 3:00 p.m. and they decided to have a nap, before they got themselves ready to go out to eat with Ricardo and Marco.

Lianne quickly fell into a deep sleep and dreamt about her father and his life in Barga. She dreamt that she was walking alongside her dad through the cobbled streets when he suddenly disappeared, leaving her on her own. She was running up and down the streets trying to find him; she would catch a glimpse of him down a side street, but she could never quite catch up with him. She woke with a start; the dream had been so vivid, that for a moment she didn't know where she was.

As her breathing slowed down, she remembered everything. Where she was, and why she had come all the way to Italy. She got up and walked into the living area, poured herself a cold glass of water and then headed for the balcony, where she sat wondering about everything that had happened in the last couple of months. She felt physically and emotionally drained; and despite being a realist, there was a degree of disappointment, that she hadn't been able to track down her father. But she hadn't and she now needed to put it all behind her and move on with her life, she needed to get back to work, and start to get back some normality.

Chapter 12

Both girls were ready when Ricardo and Marco arrived to pick them up, they both looked very smart in their blazers with open neck shirts and chinos. In fact, Lianne felt a little under dressed in her Capri pants, which she wore with flat sandals. Gemma was also wearing Capri pants, but had on a pair of unbelievably high sandals which showed off her slim ankles.

Ricardo laughed as soon as he saw them "You will—how you say—break your neck in these shoes!"

"I don't care," came the reply. "I brought them all this way, and I'm not going home unless I've worn them!" They all laughed, including Gemma, and made their way to the car.

Marco drove them out of Lucca, heading toward Santa Catarina, he then turned off the main road and down a dirt track, to a small restaurant lit with hundreds of multi coloured lights. Inside, the restaurant was a real mismatch of tables and chairs which would have driven you mad if you had a touch of OCD, but the girls found it charming and Marco assured them that it served the best food in the area. It was obviously very popular, and there were only two empty tables in the restaurant, the clientele came from far and wide for the food which was all homemade and sourced locally.

They were shown to their table, and the waitress gave them menus and highlighted the 'specials' of the day. After they'd ordered, Ricardo asked what they had got up to on their last day and Lianne explained that they'd hired a car and gone to Barga. She told them what they'd seen and what a beautiful place she thought it was.

"It was so incredibly peaceful," she said, "especially up on the top by the church. And we could see for miles, it really was spectacular. I know I didn't meet my father, but I did feel a sense of completeness, walking down the streets that my dad would have walked."

At that point, their first course arrived and the chatting stopped, while they enjoyed their food. Afterwards, the conversation was more light-hearted and they chatted easily about anything and everything. Lianne sat back in her chair, while she listened to Marco telling tales from the rugby pitch which had them in stitches at times. As she listened to Marco, Lianne couldn't help but look at Ricardo who was sitting opposite her; there was no doubt, he was a good-looking man and she could quite easily fall for him, given the chance.

"Don't be so stupid," she said to herself "the last thing you need now is a relationship with a guy who lives in a different country!" With that, she noticed that Ricardo was looking straight at her, as he smiled his whole face seemed to light up and Lianne found herself blushing. So she quickly looked away and tried to show interest in what Marco was saying, as her stomach seemed to tie itself in knots.

When they left the restaurant, they all agreed that it had been a lovely evening and the food had been exceptional. Ricardo suggested that Lianne sit in the front of the car, next to him, and that Marco sat in the back with Gemma.

"I am very sad you are going home tomorrow, Lianne. I would have liked to spend more time with you, and show you more of my country."

"I would have liked that," Lianne replied, "but I must get back to work."

"Could I please have your phone number?" Ricardo asked. "In case the boy in the shop comes back to me. Also, I come to UK several times a year, so I would like to see you if I can."

"Of course," she said, and she took a piece of paper out of her bag and wrote down her phone number. She handed Ricardo the piece of paper when he pulled up outside their apartment, and as their fingers touched, she felt something like an electric current run through her. He gently kissed both her cheeks as he said goodbye, and he held her hands in his for what seemed like an eternity; Lianne didn't want it to end, although she knew it must.

As she headed into the apartment, Lianne couldn't help but think about the irony of her meeting a handsome guy in Italy, just like her Mam had done, 30 years before. She really hoped Ricardo contacted her, but on the other hand, she knew she wasn't in the right headspace for a relationship, least of all a long distance one.

After saying their goodbyes, the girls headed up to the apartment and Lianne was suddenly aware that Gemma was talking to her. "Sorry," she said, "what did you say?"

"I said," Gemma replied, "that we need to leave here about 10:00 a.m. tomorrow, to give ourselves plenty of time to get back to the airport and check in."

"Yes, I was thinking about 10ish. I think I might pack my bag now, so I have less to do in the morning."

"Good idea," Gemma said, "how about we sort ourselves out, and then we can sit on the balcony for half an hour, and finish off the bottle of wine that's in the fridge?"

Lianne agreed that it was an excellent idea, and 20 minutes later they were doing just that.

"Are you alright?" Gemma asked. "I know this hasn't quite worked out the way you wanted it to."

"I can't deny, I had this ridiculous fantasy playing out in my head, of us walking into the ice-cream parlour, seeing Gino and then being reunited with my dad. You know what it's like—you imagine that it's all going to be so easy, just like it is on TV or in films, but in reality, it's probably impossible to track someone down, who doesn't even know I exist. So that's that, but at least I saw where my Dad lived, and where he met Mam."

"And you met Ricardo! Don't forget him, he's gorgeous!"

"True," Lianne said, "but I'm never going to see him again, am I? Let's be honest, we must live about a thousand miles apart! But he was a really nice guy and very easy to talk to. Anyway, I'm off to bed, I shall see you in the morning. Night night, and thank you so much for coming with me, it means a lot."

"No need to thank me, it was a pleasure. Try and have a good night's sleep and I'll see you in the morning."

Chapter 13

Lianne and Gemma were up early and had breakfast before throwing the last few bits into their cases. Their lift back to the airport was on time, and before they knew it, they were back in the airport. About half an hour before the girls boarded their flight, Lianne had a text from Ricardo:

**I enjoyed spending time with you and am sorry that you not find your father but hopefully you will soon.
Have a good flight and please let me know when you home safely.
Yours, Ricardo x**

"That was thoughtful of him," Gemma said.
"Yes, it was," came the reply.
The flight left on time and within a few hours, the girls were home. Lianne was curled up on the settee in her pyjamas, when she remembered that she hadn't text Ricardo back. She took out her phone and quickly fired off a text.

Both home in one piece. Thank you for your kindness over the weekend, I enjoyed spending time with you too. If you're ever in the UK it would be lovely to see you again. Lianne x

She knew it was highly unlikely that she'd see or hear from him again, but that didn't stop her from dreaming. With that she headed for bed, it had been a long day and she was exhausted; she quickly fell into a deep sleep and didn't wake at all. The next morning, the sun was streaming through the window and when she pulled back the curtains, she was almost disappointed when she didn't see Lucca stretched out before her.

But it made Lianne focus on the fact that she was back home and needed to sort things out and get back to work. She phoned her boss and had a chat about starting back, and it was agreed that she would return the following Monday. But on reduced hours for the first week or so, until she felt strong enough to commit to full time.

Knowing she was returning to work also helped to focus in other ways. She finished clearing out her Mam's stuff, finally contacted everyone that she needed to, and started to make plans to get some work done on the house. She wasn't sure if she wanted to stay in the house permanently or not, but even if she sold it, she knew she would get a far better price if work was done to update the house and freshen it up a bit.

It was later that week that Lianne heard from Ricardo again. He said that he had been invited to attend a conference in Birmingham, in about 6 weeks' time, and he wanted to know if he could see her. Lianne was a bit taken aback, she honestly hadn't expected to hear from him again, but she was secretly overjoyed. She replied saying that it would be nice to see him, however he should know that she would be back in work by then.

Ricardo assured her that was not a problem, the conference was running from Wednesday to Friday, and what he hoped to do, was to come to Cardiff on the Friday evening, and then fly home on the Monday. He asked her for the name of a hotel nearby, and Lianne responded by saying that she hoped he would stay at hers. She then quickly added that there were a number of spare bedrooms, just in case he had any funny ideas.

After that, they exchanged texts regularly, and Face-Timed each other on a number of occasions. As the date of his visit got nearer, the number of butterflies in Lianne's stomach increased dramatically. She mentioned it to Gemma a couple of weeks later, when they met up one evening after work for a quick drink. "I just can't understand it," Lianne said, "why on earth have I got butterflies!"

"I think you know why," Gemma said, "you've fallen for him, hook, line and sinker. Admit it, go on!"

"I will not! I've only known the guy for a few days!"

"Well," Gemma said, "we'll see what happens when he arrives!"

When Ricardo arrived in the UK, they chatted a number of times on the phone, and Lianne busied herself making sure the bedroom was all ready for him and generally clean. He was due to arrive at about 7:00 p.m., on the Friday, and

Lianne was getting quite worked up about him. From about 6:00 p.m., she must have tried on half a dozen different outfits—one was too formal, another too slutty—Lianne found fault in everything. Eventually, she settled on a pair of jeans and a pale lemon jumper "I might as well be comfortable," she said to herself, and headed downstairs to check on the food.

She had decided to go with a good, old fashioned Sunday roast and everything was coming together nicely. She had made an apple crumble for dessert and had bought beer and a couple of bottles of wine.

Lianne was just checking on the roast potatoes, when the doorbell rang; she quickly removed her apron and checked in the mirror that she looked OK. With that, she opened the front door and she could feel her heart pounding in her chest, as he stood before her. She couldn't get her words out either, but words were not necessary as he put his arms around her, and kissed her on both cheeks.

"Lianne, you are even more beautiful than I remember, and whatever you are cooking smell very good!"

"Please, come on in," Lianne said, as her cheeks turned red at his complement and she realised they were still standing on the doorstep. "Dinner will be ready in about 30 minutes, so there's plenty of time if you'd like to freshen up."

"That would be great, grazie. The train very busy and hot."

Lianne couldn't help but think how handsome he was in his suit, as she showed him upstairs to what had always been the spare bedroom. She had worked like crazy over the last few days, wanting to ensure that the room was spotless and had even thought about redecorating the room, but decided that was taking things a little too far! Lianne showed Ricardo where the bathroom was and left him to shower and change, whilst she went downstairs to check on the food. As she did, all she could think about was the naked man upstairs in her bathroom.

Ricardo came downstairs 20 minutes later, and looked even more handsome in a pair of Gant blue jeans and a pale-blue polo shirt, that showed off his natural tan and excellent physique. Lianne dished up the meal and they chatted easily, exchanging stories about their families and their lives. After they had finished eating, Lianne made coffee and they went and sat in the lounge.

"I find it very strange you do not know your father," Ricardo said. "I cannot imagine what you are thinking when you find letters. I come from a small family with one sister. My parents were very happy and still hold hands when out walking, until my father pass away. I also have lots of cousins and whilst it can be hard being in big family as you never have quiet, it also very good as am never alone."

"I suppose I don't know any different," Lianne replied, "it was always just me and Mam. I asked questions now and again about why I didn't have a father or siblings like my friends and I don't think my Mam ever lied to me, she just never told me the whole truth. And I suppose because I was so happy, I never pressed Mam for information."

"It must be very hard for you looking after your Mama, MND is very bad. I have patient with MND who died last year. Very sad."

"It was hard and to be honest, neither of us had really heard of MND before Mam's diagnosis. It's so awful, almost as if Mam was dying a bit at a time."

With that, a small tear appeared in the corner of her eye, Ricardo apologised for upsetting her and she assured him that he hadn't.

Lianne went on to ask if Ricardo had heard anything from the guy in the ice-cream parlour but Ricardo said he hadn't. Lianne was disappointed but knew that if she was going to hear, it would have happened by now, so that was the end of things. It just wasn't meant to be and she needed to put things into perspective.

"I'm sad, obviously, that I'm never going to meet my dad," she said, "but I think the only way to look at all this, is to remember that not having him around has never been an issue, and I actually know more about him now, than I ever did."

Ricardo agreed and the conversation moved on to other things, Lianne talked a little about her Mam, and Ricardo told her all about his family, and in particular, his nieces and nephews who he described as 'fuori di testa' or bonkers!

"I love them very much," he said, "but very happy when they go home, it very tiring being with them."

"I can imagine," Lianne said, "unfortunately I've never had that problem, my mother was an only child and so am I, so there are no nieces or nephews. But I hope one day I will settle down and have children of my own."

"I very surprised you not already married. You are very beautiful…how you say? Outside and in?"

Lianne could feel herself blushing. She told Ricardo all about Grant and how she had put her social life on hold when her Mam had been diagnosed.

"How about you?" She asked. "A handsome young doctor, how come you haven't been snapped up?"

Ricardo told her that he had been dating a girl that he had met when he was doing his medical training, they had managed to maintain a relationship despite his long hours. But when his work started to settle down and they saw more of each other, he had realised that they had very little in common and probably never would. So, he had ended the relationship and had never met anyone else.

They continued to chat well into the night and when they finally retired to their separate rooms, Ricardo held her shoulders and kissed her very gently on her lips. Lianne could feel that strange sensation throughout her body as they kissed, and that stayed with her until she fell into a deep sleep.

Chapter 14

The next morning, Ricardo found Lianne sitting at the kitchen table drinking tea when he came downstairs. She'd got up early to make sure she looked presentable; her hair often looked as if she'd been 'dragged through a hedge backwards' as her Mam used to say, and she didn't want to look like that today.

"Buongiorno bellissima signora," he said, as he walked into the kitchen. Lianne was uncertain exactly what he had said, but felt herself blushing anyway.

"Good morning," she replied. "I hope you slept OK. Can I get you some breakfast? Coffee?"

"I sleep well, thank you. Maybe toast and coffee, if this is OK."

"Of course, it is, please sit down."

Ricardo sat at the table and Lianne set about making him some breakfast. Whilst he ate, they chatted about their plans for the day, they agreed that they would head into the city centre, so that Ricardo could see Cardiff's historic castle, which dated back to Roman times and also the museum which housed some fascinating collections.

Once they arrived in the city centre, they decided to take the tour bus which drove them around all of Cardiff's main attractions, including the Bay Area, the Wales Millennium Centre, and the Principality Stadium, where the national team played its rugby. Despite having lived in Cardiff all of her life, Lianne was amazed at how little she knew about her hometown as they took in the sights.

After they had done the tour of the castle, they walked alongside the river, heading toward a small cafe. As they walked, Lianne stumbled slightly and Ricardo instantly grabbed her hand to stop her from falling. Almost immediately, she felt butterflies in her stomach and a strange sort of nervousness, but she made no attempt to remove her hand and they continued in silence until they reached the cafe. They found a table in the sunshine and ordered some drinks.

"Cardiff is beautiful city," Ricardo said. "Marco has visited many times for the rugby and I see why he keep coming."

"Cardiff is quite small in comparison to other capital cities," Lianne said, "but we have everything we need—history, culture, shops and first-class venues for concerts, theatre and the rugby of course! I do love it here."

"I understand why. I am very much liking Cardiff and its people." With that, Lianne looked away, afraid that her eyes would betray her and Ricardo would see how much she was enjoying his company too.

They finished their drinks and continued to talk as they walked; and it seemed so natural to hold hands, that neither of them was even conscious that they were. At Ricardo's request, Lianne made a reservation at her favourite restaurant, just outside Cardiff. Ricardo had said that he wanted to take her out for dinner that evening—somewhere special he had said. Caesar's, was Lianne's favourite restaurant, it served excellent food and the service was impeccable, so Lianne was surprised she could get a table, but was delighted at the same time. She had not been since her Mam had deteriorated about six months before she had passed away, so she was really looking forward to it.

They arrived back at the house at about 4:30 p.m., and Ricardo retired to his room saying that he needed to check his emails, etc. Lianne also went to her room and immediately opened her wardrobe, trying to decide what to wear that evening. She couldn't remember the last time she had bought herself clothes other than jeans and t-shirts or the stuff she wore for work.

So there was not a lot of choice, but she finally settled on a turquoise blue dress which she had had for several years, which she had only worn once or twice. She showered, did her hair and make-up and was back downstairs by 6:30 p.m.

Ricardo was waiting for Lianne when she came downstairs and she could not help but notice how handsome he looked. He was wearing a pair of navy chinos with a crisp white shirt and a blue tweed jacket. It was Ricardo who spoke first, telling Lianne how beautiful she looked. She felt herself blushing but was secretly pleased by his complement. At that moment, a text message alerted her to the arrival of their taxi and she wrapped her pashmina around her shoulders, as they headed out of the house.

They rode in the back of the taxi in almost complete silence, just holding hands and allowing their fingers to intertwine.

"You are smiling," he said.

"I'm happy," she replied, "happier than I've been in a very long time." With that, she squeezed his hand and he too smiled.

They arrived at the restaurant and were quickly shown to their table, which was in a quiet corner, away from the hustle and bustle of the kitchen. Lianne explained that she always had the same meal whenever she was lucky enough to eat at Caesar's, because she enjoyed it so much, but she was certain that whatever Ricardo went for would be delicious. They ordered their food and Ricardo ordered an expensive bottle of Italian wine to go with it.

"I know this is all happen very quickly," Ricardo said, "but I am falling very much in love with you Lianne. You truly beautiful woman both on inside and out, and I do not want to leave on Monday. I not want to ever leave you."

Lianne felt completely overwhelmed but it was the most natural thing in the world to tell Ricardo that she loved him too. What she was feeling had taken her completely by surprise. After losing her Mam, she never expected to feel this happy ever again yet she felt so happy that she was ready to burst.

"I'm obviously following in my Mam's footsteps, falling for a handsome Italian," she said with a smile. "The only difference is that I have no intention of losing you!"

"And I will not lose you either," Ricardo responded.

With that, their first course arrived. As always, the food was fabulous and they thoroughly enjoyed it. And as they ate, they chatted about their lives, getting to know each other better and their respective families.

Lianne told Ricardo all about Grant and the enormous chip on his shoulder because she had done better in her exams than him. She explained that she had owed it to her Mam to work hard at university and not take it for granted. Her Mam had worked so hard to get Lianne through her course, it would have been criminal to throw away the opportunity she had had.

"You must have been very close to your mama," Ricardo said.

"I was," she replied, "it was always just the two of us and we were really good friends, as well as mother and daughter. I miss her so much."

With that, a single tear rolled down Lianne's face and Ricardo gently wiped it away. "It's hard sometimes though. I thought we never kept secrets from one another, so you can imagine my shock when I found out about my dad. I'd never asked Mam lots of questions about him, I didn't need to, we had each other and that's all that mattered. She must have known that I'd find the letters after she'd gone, so I hope she's happy about me trying to find him—if I ever do. I had hoped that I would have heard something by now."

"Si. I hoped I hear by now, but maybe many reasons no one call. Not give up yet," he said as he squeezed her hand.

Ricardo talked more about his parents; his father had been a doctor too and always seemed to be working when Ricardo was growing up, so they had all looked forward to their family holidays at Lake Garda. They would spend 2 weeks there every summer. It was where Ricardo had learnt to swim and the one place where his father seemed to be able to relax and just be a husband and father, rather than Doctor Moretti.

His dad had been the complete opposite of his mother who had been a fairly quiet, reserved person. She was not the sort to make grand gestures but she always made sure her children knew how much they were loved and she would have done anything for them. Ricardo said he had had a wonderful childhood, despite his father's long hours and he would not have changed anything.

They drank their coffees and Lianne called for a taxi, which arrived about 20 minutes later. Once again, they said very little on the drive home, preferring to sit in silence and hold hands.

The taxi dropped them off, and as Lianne fumbled trying to get the key in the front door, she was only too aware that Ricardo was right behind her. She could smell his aftershave and feel his warm breath on her neck; the combination was resurrecting feelings her body had not felt for a very long time—if ever. Once inside the hallway, she could not resist any longer and gently kissed his lips that tasted of wine and coffee. They broke apart for a brief moment and the second kiss was more ardent, as was the third, the fourth…

They finally came up for air, both smiling and beaming with happiness. Neither spoke for what seemed like the longest time. Then as always happens, they both started to speak at the same time.

"Sorry," Ricardo said, "please you say first."

"It sounds so silly…no I can't."

"You can," Ricardo assured her, "but OK, I say first, my life change for the better the day your friend wears high heels to walk around Lucca!" They both laughed as Ricardo continued. "I love you with my heart and my soul and I want spend my life with you, I want to grow old with you."

Tears slowly traced a path down Lianne's face. "I love you too. After Mam died, I never thought I would ever be happy again. My life changed the day she died. But because of her I met you and so I know this is fate, this is what was meant to happen."

Ricardo agreed and they continued talking as Lianne made coffee, which they took into the lounge. They curled up on the sofa together and within minutes they were asleep in each other's arms.

Chapter 15

The next morning, they were both still beaming with happiness. It was a beautiful day and Lianne suggested that they head up to the Brecon Beacons so that she could show Ricardo some of the amazing countryside. And so, after they had both showered and changed, they climbed into her old Clio and headed north.

She told Ricardo all about the car, how it had been a present from her Mam, and how no man should dare suggest she get a new one!

"I'm serious," she said as Ricardo laughed, "love me, love my car! We come as a package!"

"Va bene! OK, I not say one word!"

As they headed out of the city, Lianne told Ricardo some of the history of the Valleys, of the numerous coal mines that had once created a thriving economy and brought families from all over the UK and further afield to the area.

"There were many Italians that came over here," she said, "and if you go into any of the Valley's towns you'll still find the Italian cafes and ice-cream parlours, just like Gino's."

As they passed, Aberfan Lianne talked of the tragedy that had unfolded one October day in 1966; of the colliery tip that had been created on the mountain above Aberfan and the period of heavy rain that had caused the tip to suddenly slide down the mountain engulfing the local school and several other buildings. With a tear in her eye, she told him that 116 children and 28 adults had died that day and pointed out the white arches in the Bryntaf Cemetery, which marked the graves of those children that had died. Neither of them said anything, there was nothing you could say.

The scenery slowly began to change again as they continued northward and soon all you could see was the lush green countryside and the occasional sheep. They passed the three reservoirs alongside the main road and as they headed up toward the Beacons their mood lifted. As they approached the Storey Arms, it was clear lots of other people had also planned to spend their Sunday there too.

But Lianne managed to find a parking space and they headed off toward Pen-y-fan.

There were numerous other people walking up and down the mountain on the well-worn track, but Lianne and Ricardo were oblivious to everyone else; they walked at a steady pace hand in hand, saying very little. When they finally reached the summit, the view was spectacular, it was one of those rare days when you could quite clearly see the Bristol Channel as well as the Gower Peninsula and much, much more. It truly was a beautiful place.

Lianne had packed a small picnic—some fruit, cheese, cold meat, and olives—and had several bottles of water in her rucksack. They found a relatively quiet spot looking toward Brecon itself, and sat on the grass to enjoy the view while they ate.

It was Lianne that spoke first, "What time is your flight tomorrow?"

"About half twelve," he replied, "I only carry hand luggage, so not need to be at airport until 11 o'clock."

"I can take you to the airport," she said, with a tear in her eye. "I can't believe you have to go so soon; I want to stay here with you forever."

"Me also, Mio amore. I not want to leave you ever, but we both must work so we need to make arrangements to see each other."

Lianne said that her work was flexible and with internet access she could work from almost anywhere. Ricardo was more restricted with his GP practice and he was often on call, but he tended to have every other weekend off completely. So, they could see each other for 3 or 4 days every fortnight. It certainly was not what either of them wanted, and it was not ideal, but it was probably the best they could do for the time being.

Neither of them wanted to start the climb back down the mountain, as they knew it would signal the beginning of the end of the lovely weekend they had spent together. But needs must and they slowly made their way down to the car park.

Before they knew it, they were home; Lianne made her way into the kitchen and Ricardo followed her. As she lifted up her head, the tears in her eyes were clearly visible and Ricardo kissed her forehead very gently, then her eyelids, her cheeks, and finally her mouth.

"Do not cry little one, I cannot bear to see you so sad. I know it very hard that I go tomorrow, but I be back very soon."

With that, he kissed her very gently again but her response was a lot more passionate and within moments they were climbing the stairs to her room.

"You are sure?" He asked, not wanting to take advantage of her.

"Very," came the reply.

There was nothing hurried about their lovemaking; they both wanted to savour every moment and when they were both spent, Lianne lay in his arms, running her hands across his chest. As she did so, a tear ran down her face and Ricardo felt it on his shoulder.

"You are crying again! Have I hurt you?"

"No, of course not."

"So why you cry?"

"My Mam always told me that one day I'd be so happy I'd cry. I never believed her until now."

With that, he held her tight and ran his hands across her back; she looked up at him and kissed him again and again as his hands moved further down her back to her buttocks. They made love again, exploring each other's bodies and finally fell into a deep sleep.

Chapter 16

Monday morning dawned, and they made love again before showering and getting dressed. Lianne then made them both breakfast which they ate in silence; both were dreading Ricardo returning to Italy but knew it had to be done.

They left for the airport at about 10:15 a.m. and made it in good time, Lianne thought it ironic, that if she had been a rush, every set of traffic lights would have been red but today, because she wanted to drag things out as long as possible, the roads were quiet and the lights were all green.

As Lianne dropped him off, she held on to him for as long as she possibly could; there were more tears, but this time they were tears of sadness.

"I will text when we land," Ricardo assured her, "and I Face-Time you tonight. Please do not cry."

"I'm sorry, I've only just found you and am losing you already."

"You never lose me. Lo prometto. I promise."

Lianne buried her face in his chest again and then Ricardo started to pull away. "I must go now, but I speak with you later."

They shared one final kiss and then he was gone. As he disappeared into the terminal building Lianne's tears were flowing freely and as she climbed into her car a text message through on her phone. It was from Ricardo.

I love you 🫶 🫶 xx

Lianne smiled, turned the engine on and headed home.

She was determined to keep herself busy and headed upstairs to strip the beds. As she took off the pillowcases she could smell his aftershave and Lianne held it a little closer breathing in his scent. She took the sheets downstairs and popped them in the machine, all except the one pillowcase which she held on to. She then realised that she hadn't read any of her emails since Friday lunchtime, so decided to try and do a little work.

As promised, Ricardo let her know when the flight landed and at that point Lianne relaxed a little, although she was also concerned, as before he had left, they had not made any definite plans to meet up anytime soon. The had talked about their schedules and what their options were, but nothing had been agreed. At the time, Lianne had put it down to the fact that neither of them had wanted to acknowledge that he was going to have to fly home. However, sitting in the living room on her own she wondered if maybe he had just used her. She would repeatedly go through things in her mind and would alternate between believing that he really did love her, and thinking that he had only contacted her knowing he could get her into bed and make his boring medical conference a little more interesting.

She imagined him telling Marco all about it, how he had played the game, not putting any pressure on her and within 48 hours she had succumbed to his charms. She felt so stupid, how could she be so gullible? She had never jumped into bed with a guy so quickly in her life. In fact, other than Grant she had only ever slept with one other man.

All these thoughts were going through her head and she realised it was absolutely pointless trying to work, she must have read the same email at least 20 times and still didn't have a clue what it said. It was nearly 5:00 p.m. by then, and so she decided to text Gemma.

'Do u fancy a glass of wine after work? Think I've done something stupid. Flying horse at 6.30? xx'

The reply came through a few moments later.

'Sounds good to me. Will make a change from me being stupid 😄 😄 see you there xx'

Lianne went and had another shower, feeling as if she needed to clean every trace of him off her. By now, she had concluded that she had jumped into bed with him so quickly because she was still grieving. It was as if she needed to have some excuse for her behaviour and that made perfect sense, she had decided. She felt a little better having come up with a reason for such wanton behaviour and was a little brighter when she arrived at the Flying Horse. She ordered 2 large glasses of white wine and found a quiet corner to wait.

Gemma arrived a few minutes late, apologising profusely and waffling on about her boss who had apparently completely changed his mind about a piece of work he had asked her to do.

"Anyway, enough about me. Spill the beans, what have you done?"

"I slept with Ricardo," came the reply. "I was taken in by all his suave Italian sexiness and I slept with him."

"Is that all! Bloody hell Li, I thought you'd done something really stupid! Anyway, when did this happen? I was with you nearly all the time we were in Lucca, did he sneak over after I'd gone to bed?" Gemma laughed. If jumping into bed with some sweet-talking guy was stupid, she was obviously stupid quite frequently.

"No, not over there." Lianne replied and went on to explain everything that had happened over the weekend. "He said he loved me, and I believed him, I can't believe I was so gullible. It's the oldest trick in the book!"

"OK, that's fair enough," Gemma said, "but what has he now done to make you think he didn't mean it?"

Lianne went to answer but then stopped. She realised he had not actually done anything. In fact, he had text her when he had landed just like he had promised he would. His only crime was that he had not contacted her since then—a matter of a few hours.

"I've overreacted, haven't I?" Gemma nodded. "He hasn't done anything wrong has he?" Gemma nodded again. "I'm a bloody idiot, aren't I?"

Gemma laughed and Lianne started to laugh too. "You're bonkers Li, you really are! Right, my round same again?" Lianne nodded and Gemma headed for the bar, as she did, Lianne's phone pinged—it was a text from Ricardo.

'So sorry, been crazy since I get back. Heading home now, Face-Time you in an hour? Miss you 💝 xx'

As Gemma walked back from the bar with 2 more glasses of wine, she saw Lianne smiling as she responded to his text message.

"That's him, isn't it?" She said with a laugh. "Oh my God, you're in love!" Lianne could not help but smile at her dearest friend, "Yes, I do believe I am!"

Chapter 17

When Ricardo Face-Timed Lianne later that evening, he explained that he had called into the surgery on his way from the airport, some test results had come in for one of his younger patients quicker than he had expected. They were not good and so he had spent the afternoon with the child's parents discussing treatment options. He apologised profusely for not having contacted Lianne sooner, but said that from the moment he had read the test results his whole focus had been on his patient and their family. Lianne told him that he had nothing to apologise for, it just showed her what a wonderful, considerate person he was and that it was one of the reasons why she loved him. He said that she must have thought that he was some kind of lothario and had not meant a word that he had said all weekend.

"Of course not!" She said with her fingers crossed. "I knew you must be busy, and I've been busy too!" She continued, all the time thinking what a terrible liar she was. She went on to tell him that she had done some work that afternoon and then met Gemma for a drink, she said nothing about her earlier doubts and he said that she had not mentioned previously that she was meeting Gemma, so was everything OK; she blamed it all on her dearest friend who was supposedly having more 'man' troubles and Ricardo laughed.

They continued to talk for over an hour, and tentatively Lianne turned the conversation around to them seeing each other again.

"I have a plan!" He announced. He explained that because he had just got back, he had a lot of work to catch up on and would be on call the following weekend. He also wanted to spend some time with his young patient and do a little digging of his own to find the right specialist.

"So," he went on, "I think maybe you come here the following weekend. There's a flight on Thursday evening, I would work Friday but finish lunchtime so we can have several days together. Would that work for you?" He asked.

When she said yes, without trying to sound too keen, he said, "I hope you say this, as I have bought ticket!"

"You didn't need to do that," she said, "I could have bought my ticket, I will give you the money when I see you."

"No, no!" He responded, "I buy ticket to make sure you come!" And he laughed. Lianne laughed too and all her doubts and concerns vanished into thin air, she obviously meant as much to him as he did to her.

Lianne let it slip that it was her birthday in a couple of days and Ricardo said that she was naughty and should have told him whilst he was in Cardiff.

"We will celebrate your birthday when you come to Lucca," he announced. "I know it be hard to enjoy your birthday, but we must celebrate." Lianne nodded and said OK.

As their conversation finally came to an end, he reminded her that he was very much in love with her and that he would speak to her the following day.

Lianne almost floated upstairs to bed, she was so happy that she could barely think straight and as she climbed into bed, she held the pillowcase to her face breathing in his scent, falling asleep within minutes.

Lianne was a lot more settled over the following days, they Face-Timed every evening and talked about their day and their plans for her visit. He was quite nervous when he had asked her if she was comfortable staying at his place or whether she wanted to stay in a hotel. She could see the look of relief on his face when she said she would stay anywhere, as long as she was with him. Her birthday came and went, it was her first without her Mam, and it felt very strange; she didn't really want to do anything and just wanted to spend the day quietly. She had a few cards and Gemma bought her an Italian phrase book.

"If you're gonna date an Italian doctor, you need to know the language!" She said with a laugh, as they tucked into the Chinese takeaway, Gemma had insisted they share.

"I guess so!" Lianne said. She'd said she wanted to be on her own, but if she was honest, she was relieved that Gemma had insisted on coming over. They drank a couple of bottles of wine with their meal and it had been good to think of something other than her Mam for a few hours.

When she walked through, into the arrivals hall at Pisa airport just a few days later, Ricardo greeted her with a massive bouquet of red roses. She almost ran into his arms and they held each other close for what seemed like an eternity; neither spoke, there was no need for words.

The drive to his apartment seemed to take forever and as they finally got inside, he scooped her up in his arms and carried her to his bedroom which smelled of his cologne. He lay her on the bed and slowly undressed her, savouring every moment and when she lay there in just the briefest of lace panties, he covered her in gentle kisses as he undressed himself. He stroked the inside of her thigh, barely touching her, until she was almost screaming with desire. He removed the piece of lace that lay between them and entered her with such passion that she climaxed almost immediately.

It was now her turn to pleasure him and she rolled him over so that he lay on his back, she teased with her tongue as she kissed every inch of him, and as she did so she heard him moan with pleasure. After a few moments when she knew it was time, she straddled him and forced herself down on him, riding him as he came inside her. And when they were done, she lay down next to him with the biggest smile on her face that he had ever seen. And then he suddenly saw a single tear run down her cheek.

"Happy tears?" He asked.

"Definitely!" Came the reply.

He smiled with relief and held her close; they lay there for some time, neither saying a word, there was no need.

On the Friday morning, Ricardo had to work, he told Lianne to help herself to anything that she could find, and that he would be home about 2:00 p.m. She lay in bed for a while after he had gone, but her stomach was rumbling and she needed food; they had not got around to eating the night before, and she was ravenous. She wandered into the kitchen and found some cereal, there was no fresh milk but she spotted a yogurt in the fridge which she had with her cereal. It was fairly obvious that Ricardo didn't do much cooking, so she decided that she would go for a wander, after she had showered, to stock up with some essentials.

Ricardo lived outside the walled city of Lucca where property prices were considerably cheaper, it seemed to be a nice enough residential area and Li didn't have to walk far before she found some local shops. She bought some fresh bread for their lunch and various cheeses and meats, as well as an array of salad vegetables and fruit. She also bought some fresh milk, fruit juice, and a bottle of wine. She decided that she would prepare lunch for when Ricardo came home from work. There was a lovely veranda off the main living area of the apartment and it was a beautiful day, perfect for a picnic for two.

Carrying the shopping back was hard, even though it was not that hot. By the time she got back and put everything away, she was exhausted. She had just sat down with a cold glass of juice, when her phone pinged, it was Ricardo.

'Missing you xx'

'Miss you too xx' she replied.

She finished her drink and went out on to the veranda; it was not big but there was a small table and a couple of chairs. They looked like they could do with a good wash, so she fetched some soapy water and a cloth. She washed them all down and rinsed them off leaving them to dry in the sunshine while she went in to start preparing lunch.

When Ricardo returned just before 2:00 p.m. everything was ready. She greeted him with a kiss and told him to take his jacket off and take a seat on the veranda, where there was a bottle of wine chilling. She poured them both a glass and produced plate after plate of food, which he devoured, unlike her, he hadn't had anything to eat, so he was hungry.

"I get very used to this," he said, kissing her cheek. "I am lucky man to have a beautiful woman who feeds me too!"

They finished the wine and ate nearly everything she had bought. They sat quietly looking out over the houses, toward the mountains, absorbing the sights and sounds of the afternoon. They could hear the traffic below, as commuters made their way home for the weekend and the chatter of children, happy to have left school behind for a few days.

There was no awkward silence between them, both felt entirely comfortable with the other and didn't feel the need to make small talk. Ricardo took her by the hand and said he was going to take a shower; he kissed her hand and went inside.

Lianne stayed on the balcony for a few minutes. She heard the water running and went inside, discarding her clothes as she headed toward the bathroom. He was singing softly and had his eyes closed as she stepped in behind him.

"You missed a bit," she said, putting her arms around him. She ran her hands across his chest and down toward his thighs, she could hear him moan as she touched him and his body made it clear how much he wanted her. He turned around to face her, kissing her with such passion, he let his hands linger on her breasts, her nipples hardening beneath his fingers. Her body was also betraying her desire and as he slid his fingers between her thighs she moaned softly. He pressed her body against the wall and took her there as the warm water continued to cascade over their entwined bodies.

When they were done, he wrapped her in a large white towel and carried her to his bed. She had never felt such desire as she did with him and she experienced wave after wave of ecstasy even before he entered her again. And finally, they both lay on the bed exhausted and drifted off to sleep.

They woke an hour or so later, and finished off the rest of the food that Li had bought that morning. They sat on the veranda for hours talking about anything and everything.

"Is there anything you like to do tomorrow?" He asked as he opened a bottle of wine. "I thought maybe we go to Florence. It take about an hour to drive, would you like to do this?"

"I would love to go to Florence, I hadn't realised it was so close. It's supposed to be a beautiful city and it's also one of the fashion capitals of the world, somewhere I read about when I was studying. It would be amazing to see it for myself. Blimey, I take you to the Brecon Beacons and you take me to Florence! There's no comparison!"

He laughed and pointed out that beauty had many forms and that he had loved being in the mountains with her.

"OK," he added, "we will leave here at 8:00 a.m. tomorrow so we spend the whole day in the city. So, we had better get some sleep!" And with that he took her hand and led her back to the bedroom.

Chapter 18

The following morning, they headed east out of Lucca toward Florence. Ricardo explained that it would be too late to get tickets to some of the more popular attractions, as these were often sold out well in advance, but they could walk through the historic centre of the city and absorb the atmosphere.

They parked on the outskirts of the city and used the tram network to get into the centre. Lianne was amazed at the sheer number of people around.

"There more visitors than residents," Ricardo told her. "Especially in summer months. Very busy." They walked for a couple of hours, and eventually stopped at a busy cafe bar to get a drink.

Lianne was still astounded at the sheer number of people around, but Ricardo pointed out that there was a downside to tourism too. Certain areas were plagued by pickpockets who took advantage of unsuspecting tourists and ruined many a holiday by stealing cash and credit cards. The tourists too, were inconsiderate, leaving litter strewn across areas where they had stopped to have a drink or eat a sandwich. They would simply move on to the next site, leaving their bottles and packaging behind them.

But despite its issues, Lianne could not help but be impressed by what she saw. They went to Santa Maria del Fiore, and were in awe of the beautiful domed cathedral. The Piazza Della Signoria with the Fountain of Neptune, which took her breath away; and the Ponte Vecchio which she must have seen a hundred times in photos, but seeing it in real life was something else. All these places that she had heard of, and seen photos of, were suddenly there before her; it had been an amazing day.

They left Florence early evening, and headed back to Lucca, they were both tired but realised that they had not eaten properly since breakfast. Ricardo said there was a small restaurant near his apartment where they could go.

"It's fairly basic," he said, "so no need to change. But they do amazing pasta and serve some good wine." It sounded perfect to Lianne, and they got there at about 9:30 p.m. having left the car at the apartment, and walking the 5 minutes to the restaurant. It was just as Ricardo described, with an odd assortment of tables and chairs, but it was busy, which was always a good sign.

The owner greeted Ricardo like a long-lost friend and he showed them to a small table towards the rear of the restaurant. He spoke to Ricardo and Li in Italian, assuming that she spoke the language. Ricardo must have pointed out that she only spoke English, as he addressed her apologetically.

"Mis cusi, Signoria. Welcome. Please you choose anything you like; I make especially for you and Doctor Moretti." With that, he handed them simple menus and disappeared into the back.

"An old friend?" Li asked.

"No," came the reply. "I was doctor for his mother, she die last year but Giuseppe always very grateful. I—how you say—make plans. So, she at home with Giuseppe when it happens. I do very little so not want him to feel grateful."

"You may not think you did a lot, but it meant a lot to him. I know when my Mam was ill, she was adamant that she wanted to die at home, not in a hospital. Doctor Richards made all the arrangements so that could happen, and I'll always be grateful to him for that, so don't underestimate what you did."

Before Ricardo could reply, Giuseppe returned with a bottle of wine, which he knew was one of Ricardo's favourites and he took their orders.

When the food arrived about 20 minutes later, they both realised how ravenous they were, and the food really was very good. They had both opted for pasta and ordered some homemade ice-cream afterwards. They finished the bottle of wine and Ricardo paid the bill before they headed back to the apartment.

Despite the fact that they were both exhausted, they sat up talking until the early hours, Lianne spoke of her grandparents who had died before she was born. Everything she knew about them were either things her Mam had told her or Diane, and none of it was very complementary.

"I can't help but wonder what would have happened if Mam had told Alfonso about me, maybe I would have grown up in Italy rather than Wales. How could they have been so heartless? Mam never spoke about them with any fondness and my Mam's cousin Diane doesn't really have anything nice to say about them. I honestly think Mam was determined to be the sort of mother she'd wished she'd had, rather than the one she did have. She really was an amazing person. I wish you could have met her. But I can't help but think that things could have been so different… "

"This is true, but if you not come looking for your father with Gemma, I not have met you. And I very happy I met you." With that, he kissed her with such tenderness that she felt as if her heart would burst. He took her hand and they headed to bed.

The next morning Lianne woke first after a restless night, she had had strange dreams about her father not wanting her and she was anxious to wake herself up properly. She jumped in the shower and then set about making some breakfast for them both.

It was another beautiful day and Ricardo had suggested that they stay close to home and maybe head out to see Marco, they could have lunch out and then a quiet evening, before normality resumed on Monday morning.

It was lovely to see Marco again although he was clearly shocked to see Li on Ricardo's arm.

"This is why I no see my friend!" He joked before embracing her and kissing her cheek. "You have capture his heart! I not think anyone ever would! welcome, welcome!" They headed to a local cafe bar and sat outside in the sunshine.

"He very happy," Marco said, while Ricardo went in to order some drinks. "After you went he very sad and keep talking about beautiful Welsh girl! So, he now very happy he see you." Li blushed and at that point Ricardo returned.

"What have you said Marco? You upset Lianne?"

"No, no!" came the reply "I just say if she get tired of being with fancy doctor I am not having a girlfriend!" With that, they all laughed and Ricardo told Marco about the medical conference and how he had met up with Li afterwards. They chatted for an hour or so and then Ricardo and Li headed further out into the country, eventually stopping at a small family restaurant, which had the most amazing views over the Tuscan countryside.

They eventually made their way back to Lucca, and Li packed her few bits and pieces into a small suitcase. Ricardo was going to take her to the airport first thing in the morning, having rearranged his morning surgery. They were both very quiet all evening, both dreading her return home and the wait then until they could meet up again.

After they had made love, they lay quietly snuggled up together and just as she was falling off to sleep, Ricardo said that he wanted to introduce Li to his mother and sister next time she came over.

"This is, OK?" He asked. "It not too soon?"

"I would love to meet your family," she replied, with a smile on her face. It was clear to her that Ricardo was as committed to this relationship as she was. And with that thought, she fell into a deep sleep.

Chapter 19

The next ten days or so passed slowly, Li tried to keep herself busy with work but it was difficult, when she lived for their conversations every evening. There had been one or two occasions when he had been late Face-Timing her, but she no longer worried. She had accepted that he was a doctor and that meant there were times when he had to put his patients first. She wouldn't expect anything less from him, and it was one of the many things she loved about him.

Finally, Li found herself on the Thursday flight back to Ricardo, as before, he was waiting for her in the arrivals hall and scooped her up in his arms.

"La mia bella ragazza," he said as he squeezed her tight—my beautiful girl. "I am missing you so much."

They headed back to his apartment and Ricardo proudly showed her that he had cleared out some drawers for her, and made some space in the wardrobe. Li was over the moon as he said, "This now your apartment too!"

As before, Ricardo worked on the Friday morning and Lianne did some food shopping, they had a quiet lunch when he got home and then went for a long walk before returning to shower and change. They went out for a lovely meal and then headed back to the apartment, where they made love.

Afterwards, Lianne tentatively asked if they were going to see his family over the weekend, she was a little worried that he may have changed his mind.

"Si, si," he replied, "I forget I not tell you. I arrange we have lunch with my Mama tomorrow, then my sister will come in the afternoon with her three bambinos. So, you meet them all!"

Despite the fact that Lianne had known that this was what he had intended she couldn't help but worry. What if they did not like her? Maybe they would think he was crazy to get involved with some mad Welsh woman! They might think she was after his money, after all he was a doctor! All these thoughts were running through her head and it was as if Ricardo could read her mind. He assured her that they would love her just as much as he did, but that didn't stop her from worrying.

Li was restless most of the night, and Ricardo found her sitting on the veranda when he woke up. She was drinking coffee and trying to stop this awful sickie feeling in her stomach, he came up behind her and placed his hands on her shoulders. He kissed the top of her head saying, "Ti Amo." I love you.

"I love you. My mother will love you and my sister," he continued "You must not worry, you will get how you say 'la ruga'—the wrinkles!" She couldn't help but laugh and promptly chased him back into the apartment. They ended up in the bedroom and he showed her how much he really loved her.

By noon, Li had tried on several different outfits; she wanted to be comfortable but respectful, not tarty but not too formal. In the end, she settled on a pair of white Capri pants and a lime green short sleeved shirt, which came down over her hips. She had washed her hair and styled it in a loose plait; she had applied her makeup and reapplied her makeup, and finally she was ready.

"You look beautiful," he said, "you always do." And then as an after-thought he added, "Bring a bathing costume!" The latter sent Li into even more of a panic, but finally, she was ready for anything!

They headed out of Lucca toward Vecchiano, where his mother lived. Ricardo explained that it was where he had been born and grown up, his father had been a GP there and had always hoped that Ricardo would follow in his footsteps. He always wanted his son to be a doctor and had been a little disappointed when Ricardo had chosen to stay in Lucca rather than return to Vecchiano, but he was incredibly proud of him.

Unfortunately, his father had died when Ricardo was in his mid-20s. He had been killed late one night whilst making a house call. His mother had never quite recovered and Ricardo was eternally grateful that his sister lived close by with her husband and three children, which kept his mother busy.

"I just thought," Li suddenly said, "does your Mam speak English? I can't speak a word of Italian! I really must learn you know! Oh, this is going to be awful—your Mam's not going to understand a word I say! She'll probably be saying all these terrible things about me in Italian and I won't have a clue what she's saying. It's going to be…" Ricardo finally managed to get a word in, "She speak very good English, and will love you, just like me!"

The house was not what Lianne had expected. For some reason, she had assumed that his mother would be in an older property, but instead Ricardo pulled up on to the driveway of a more modern bungalow. It was white with fuchsia coloured bougainvillea growing along the one wall. Before Ricardo had switched off the engine, his mother appeared at the front door, again she was totally not what Lianne had expected. No little grey-haired lady all in black; instead, a slim, attractive woman in her late-50s with white hair that was tied back into an elegant chignon. She wore apricot-coloured shorts and a coordinating sleeveless blouse.

"Ciao! Benvenuto! Welcome, welcome!" She rushed forward embracing Lianne saying, "Ricardo, Lianne far more beautiful than you say!" At that, Lianne blushed. "I am Sofia, I am so happy to meet you. Ricardo talk about you all the time!" With that, she threw her hands up in the air and kissed her son on both cheeks. "Come, come!"

Sofia led them inside to an open plan living area with patio doors that led into the rear courtyard. There was a barbecue area to the one side under cover, and a beautiful pergola again covered in bougainvillea, under which was a small dining table and four chairs. There was a small swimming pool and an array of sun loungers dotted around, and in another covered area a number of children's pedal bikes, a sandpit, and other toys. She could also see that through a wrought iron gate there was an array of flowers and what appeared to be vegetables growing.

"Wow," was all Lianne could say, "this is fantastic and so beautiful!"

"Grazie. Ricardo's papa and I move here 13 years ago, we love the space and that there no steps!" She laughed. "Steps not good for…um…ginocchia…" she looked at Ricardo, "…the knees!"

Sofia invited Li to sit under the pergola and told Ricardo to fetch the wine. They chatted for about half an hour, talking about Lianne's Mam and Ricardo's dad, and they shared photographs. Sofia then disappeared inside and returned with lasagne, and a variety of salads which she had prepared. They continued talking as they ate, and it was clear that Ricardo had told Sofia about Lianne's search for her father.

"It must be very hard," she said, "not knowing who your father is. Ricardo tell me you know nothing of him until after your mama pass away, must be big shock."

"We've heard nothing from my father's cousin," Lianne said, "so I don't think we will now. He either doesn't know where my father is or my father doesn't want to see me." There was real sadness in her voice and it was clear that she was very upset by the lack of contact.

"Please, no worry," Sofia said, "Italian men very slow!" And with that she laughed, got up and kissed Lianne's forehead and then started to clear the table.

"Please let me," Lianne said, but Sofia was adamant that she didn't need help. She returned about 5 minutes later with a selection of fresh fruit, some cheeses and a chocolate mousse, that was heavenly.

The three of them chatted easily for some time, and then the peace was suddenly shattered by shouts of "Nonna, Nonna!" Three mini human dynamos, and one of the canine variety, came charging through the house and into the courtyard. "Nonna, nonna possiamo andare a nuotare?" They all shouted.

"Si, si," came the reply. The three of them immediately started to take all their clothes off, until they were standing stark naked in front of them. The dog seemed to understand Italian perfectly, and had already launched himself into the pool.

At this point, their mother appeared. "Onestamente, voi tre mi fate impazzire! Cosa ti ho detto in macchina? Devi prima salutare l'amico di Ricardo's!" With that, the three of them stood still and said in unison, "Hello Lianne, welcome to Italy." No sooner had they finished saying their carefully rehearsed speech that they started jumping around again, so they didn't hear Lianne thank them.

Sofia got up and carefully herded the three of them back inside to find their bathing costumes. "Hello, I am Isabella," their mother said. "I apologise for my children!" But Lianne just laughed.

"They're amazing," she said.

Ricardo explained that Isabella was his older sister and was married to Emilio, the children were, Lucia aged 5, and the twins, Maria and Enzo, aged 3. The dog was Coco. At that point, all three reappeared, closely followed by their Nonna. The twins had their armbands on and all three ran headlong into the pool to join Coco, and promptly began splashing around.

"Vino per favore!" Isabella said, with an air of desperation and even Lianne understood that. Ricardo grabbed another bottle of wine from the fridge and the four adults sat under the pergola, watching the children play as that chatted. Isabella explained that she was a primary school teacher and that she had met Emilio when he had come to do some work on the school. They had been married for nearly 10 years and it had taken a long time before Lucia came along, so it was a real shock when she fell pregnant with the twins. She had recently gone back to work, and the twins were either in nursery or with their Nonna.

Lianne was completely taken aback by how open and honest Ricardo's family were with her, they were so welcoming that she felt as if she'd known them for years. Sofia then suggested that they might all like a swim and she showed Lianne through to the guest room so that she could change. "We are really very pleased to meet you," she said, "Ricardo is very happy and this is because of you."

"I love Ricardo very much," Lianne replied, "and I am so lucky to have found him."

"He very lucky also," Sofia said as she left Lianne to change.

The next couple of hours were spent in and around the pool. Emilio appeared shortly after 5:00 p.m. and whilst his English was very limited; he also made Lianne feel very welcome.

A little while later, Emilio fired up the barbecue in what was obviously a regular occurrence. Sofia brought plates of meat from the kitchen, more salads and plenty of delicious white bread. The five adults and three children ate until they were fit to burst, and it was clear that the children were getting tired. Isabella packed up her family and they headed out to the car; the children were already falling asleep in the back. She hugged Lianne tightly and told her again how pleased she was to finally meet her, she then jumped in the car and they headed off.

After Isabella and the family had gone, the others returned to the courtyard. Sofia offered them another glass of wine and Ricardo hesitated, knowing he had already had a few glasses.

As if reading his mind, Sofia asked them if they would like to stay overnight, Ricardo looked at Lianne who nodded. "Of course," Sofia said, with a glint in her eye. "I only have one bed, so you will have to share!" They all laughed, and Sofia poured more wine.

She asked Lianne about her Mam, saying that she remembered her husband having a patient with MND and what an awful disease it was. Lianne spoke of the special relationship she had had with her Mam, how her grandparents had died before she was born and so it was just the two of them. She talked about growing up, going to university and how hard her mother had worked to ensure she had everything she needed. As she did a small tear fell and Sofia took her hand saying "Your Mama be very proud of you and she always watching over you." At that, the floodgates opened and she could hardly speak, she felt so embarrassed crying in front of Sofia, but something in Sofia's eyes told her not to worry.

Shortly before 10:00 p.m. Sofia announced that she was off to bed, she had left towels, etc in the guest room and she would see them in the morning. Lianne and Ricardo were not far behind her and cuddled up together, falling asleep quickly afterwards.

In the morning, Sofia prepared a lovely breakfast for them and then they headed back to Lucca. Lianne was genuinely sorry to say goodbye, Sofia had been so welcoming that she already felt as if she was part of the family.

The rest of the weekend was spent quietly; they walked and talked and before long, Monday morning had arrived, and Lianne headed home.

Chapter 20

Lianne and Ricardo's life quickly fell into a routine; every other weekend Lianne would fly out to see him, and in between, they made do with regular Face-Time sessions. When she was with him, they filled their days with fairly mundane stuff, they would walk a lot and visit his family, they shopped together and cooked meals. In many ways, because their time together was limited, they were able to focus more easily on each other, and life's necessities such as, paying bills and visiting the dentist were banished to those times, when they were on their own.

As the summer ended and the number of tourists lessened, they had more chance to visit some of the sights. They went back to Florence in late September to see all the places they had not seen previously; and they went to places such as Pisa and Bologna where they enjoyed themselves, exploring together.

Nothing had been heard about Lianne's father and she had come to terms with the fact that he did not want anything to do with her, she had Ricardo and his family which was now her family too. Lianne and Ricardo had even started to talk about the future long term. Lianne had discussed her options with her boss, working from Italy was not too big a problem, provided she could travel if needed. So much of Lianne's job was done on computer, that she could be more or less anywhere, provided there was a wi-fi connection.

And so, Lianne and Ricardo talked about her relocating to Italy in the new year, it would give her time to sell the house and make all the necessary arrangements. She also wanted to learn Italian, as she was very conscious that she could not rely on others being able to speak English when she was living there.

It was a quiet Wednesday morning in early November, and Lianne was looking at various 'teach yourself Italian' courses when her phone pinged. It was Ricardo, which Lianne thought a little strange, as they rarely messaged in the day because of work commitments. The text simply said:

You free for FaceTime? xx

Lianne quickly replied that she was, wondering what was going on. He came through on Face-Time a few moments later; Ricardo looked really serious and Lianne could not help but worry.

"What on Earth has happened?" She asked, "Is it Sofia?"

"No, no," came the reply "I have just had a telephone call from a man called Francesco Piacentini—your fathers brother." Li looked confused. "Apparently, Gino took my card and put it in pocket then forgot about it. He find card a few days ago and speak to grandfather who speak to Francesco. He very shocked because he know nothing of you, so I explain you know nothing until your Mama pass away. He remember Alfonso talking about your Mama many, many years ago but no more. Are you OK?"

Lianne was literally sat there open mouthed, unable to take in everything she was hearing. "It's crazy it's been more than 6 months since we gave that guy the card. I'd assumed that he'd either thrown it away or my dad didn't want anything to do with me. I'd honestly given up on hearing from anyone. I'm just shocked!"

"That is to be expected. I had shock when he tell me who he is on phone. I tell him you will be in Lucca end of next week, he would like to meet you. Do you want to do this?"

"Has he said anything about my dad?" She asked.

"No," he replied, "he said he like to meet you first."

Lianne seemed a little puzzled "I wonder why? Maybe he's dead too." And with that, a tear ran down her face.

"We not know this Lianne. There many reasons why Francesco want to meet you first, please do not worry. Are you happy if I ring him and make arrangements?"

"Yes," she replied.

They spoke for another few minutes and then Ricardo said he had to get back to work and that he would Face-Time her again that evening. Lianne sat on the settee not knowing what to think or do, she was completely at a loss. Eventually she made herself a coffee and text her Mam's cousin Diane, it simply said:

Are you home? Could do with a chat xx

About 15 minutes later, Lianne got the answer she had hoped for, she grabbed her bag and jumped in the car.

"I have to admit," Diane said, "I'd assumed that you'd got nowhere trying to track your dad down."

"I'd honestly given up too. For the first couple of weeks, I'd expected Ricardo to ring me and say that my dad had been found, but when that didn't happen I just assumed that he wanted nothing to do with me because Mam hadn't told him about me. But now I don't know what to think. Dad's brother Francesco hasn't said anything about my dad. So I don't know what the situation is, but I'm meeting him next week, Ricardo is arranging it. I presume I'll know more then. Oh my God I'm actually terrified!"

Diane moved to sit next to Lianne and she put her arm around her shoulders. "Listen love, there's absolutely nothing to worry about. What's the worst that can happen? Your dad decides he doesn't want anything to do with you—if that happens, you're no worse off than you are now. But to be honest, I can't ever imagine your Mam having fallen in love with someone who would behave like that. But if it happens, it happens, and at the end of the day you'll still have your Ricardo. Now I want to know all about him!"

Lianne smiled; Diane was right; she had managed up to now without a dad. And as long as she had Ricardo she would be just fine. "So, let me tell you about Ricardo—he is amazing…"

Chapter 21

Just over a week later Lianne boarded her flight; despite the reassurances from Ricardo every night, she was still very apprehensive about meeting Francesco. As always, Ricardo was waiting in the arrivals hall when she'd cleared customs and he could see straight away how anxious she was. He tried to keep the conversation light-hearted as they drove to his apartment, but it was clear the she could think of nothing other than meeting Francesco the following day. It was arranged that they would meet on the Friday afternoon at a cafe bar in Lucca, not far from the ice-cream parlour.

They spent the evening quietly and were both in bed early, although neither got much sleep, as Lianne was very restless.

Ricardo went to work as usual on the Friday morning and Lianne went and did a little food shopping, after she had showered. It was as if she was working on auto pilot, she went to the usual place and bought the usual things, knowing that Ricardo would need some lunch before they went into Lucca. Not that she could face eating, her stomach was in knots.

Lianne returned to the apartment, and once again set about trying to decide what to wear, she had been through this whole process numerous times when she was back home, and had brought several different combinations with her in her hand luggage, plus there were clothes that she left in Ricardo's apartment permanently. After trying on various outfits, she was no more certain. "Bloody ridiculous," she said out loud, "I can't even sort out what to wear! I'm useless!" After more indecision, she finally decided on the same outfit she had chosen when she was back home, a pair of jeans and an apricot-coloured jumper, which she lay out across the bed.

Ricardo returned for lunch and she dished up some soup and fresh bread, he could see how nervous she was, as she simply moved the spoon around the bowl but was not actually eating anything. "Francesco will love you, you be fine, but now please try eat something or you…faint!"

Lianne smiled, and ate a little before going through to change, she returned about 20 minutes later. "Bellisimo," was all that Ricardo said.

It was late November, and there was a definite chill in the air; Ricardo parked the car and led Lianne through the narrow streets to the cafe bar, where they would meet Francesco.

"We are early," Ricardo said as they stepped inside, "so please no worry if he not here yet." But literally as he said it, a chap in his late-40s stood at a table in the corner.

He took Lianne's hand and kissed it tenderly. "I find old photographs of Alfonso and your Mama and I see you very beautiful, like her. Mi scusi, Doctor Moretti, it is good to meet you too."

The three of them sat, and Francesco called over a waiter who took their order, none of them spoke for a few moments and then Francesco spoke.

"I very sorry hear of Maggie's death. Alfonso say she was a very special girl and she stole his heart. Please you tell me what happened."

Lianne started from the beginning, she explained that she had never wondered who her father was, she had her Mam, and everything she needed. She went on to tell him how her Mam's cousin Diane had filled her in on what had happened after her Mam had passed away, and she had found the letters. She opened her handbag and placed the letters, which were tied neatly together with ribbon, on the table.

"As you can imagine, I was completely shocked when I found them and had never heard of Alfonso. But my Mam obviously wanted me to find them," she said. "Otherwise she could have easily destroyed them before she got sick."

She went on to explain how she'd travelled to Italy with her friend after her Mam had passed away in the hope of retracing her Mam's footsteps. She said she'd found the ice-cream parlour quite by chance, but had been saddened to hear that Gino was dead.

"Gino was good friend to Alfonso, but he like fun, not want to study. He die in accident when he about 20 and there no real contact with his girlfriend or son after."

"That's tragic," Lianne said, "from what was written in Alfonso's letters to my Mam, they were very close."

"What I not understand," Francesco said. "Why Maggie no tell Alfonso that she have baby."

"I think she wanted to, but from what I have been told, she was worried that a pregnant girlfriend would mean the end of his career. She knew he intended to go to university and study architecture. My grandparents had died not long after she met Alfonso, so she knew she could manage financially for a little while at least. She didn't want a summer romance to ruin his life."

"I think she very brave and must have love Alfonso very much."

Lianne nodded, "I think so too."

Ricardo had said little up to this point but now felt the need to ask. "I must ask, is Alfonso still alive? Because you wanted to meet, Lianne very worried."

"Scusi. Alfonso is OK, he live in Bologna now." Lianne breathed a sigh of relief and Francesco could clearly see the relief on her face. "I ask to meet you, to see you, you are…" he looked directly at Ricardo "genuina, you understand? Alfonso, he lose his wife last year and I not want upset him. I needed to know you not hurt him but I see you very kind person like your Mama."

"So, what happens now?" Lianne asked. "Will you tell him about me and ask if he wants to meet me? I understand that he may decide that he doesn't want to acknowledge me, as I know it would create a lot of problems for him, and I accept that. I just need to know."

"I go see Alfonso, it not good to speak on the phone about such things."

"Si," Ricardo said. "I agree not good to tell him on phone."

"Would you give him these please Francesco?" Lianne said, reaching into her handbag again. She pulled out two photos, one of her Mam holding her when she was a few months old and another taken of them both at her graduation. They both looked so well and happy in the latter.

Francesco took the photographs from her. "Your Mama very beautiful girl and I see she was very beautiful woman. I ring Alfonso tonight and see him as soon as I can. I will let you know when that happen and what he say."

"I cannot thank you enough," Lianne said, taking Francesco's hand, "this means so much to me, grazie."

They continued talking for a little while longer and then they left. It was getting dark as they stepped back out on to the streets of Lucca and there were Christmas lights hung from everywhere, it was truly beautiful and quite magical. Lianne was so relieved that her dad was still alive, but she was realistic about things. Accepting Lianne as his daughter could cause so many problems for him.

"I didn't ask him," she suddenly said, all excited. "I didn't ask if I have brothers or sisters!"

"There is plenty time to ask such questions, mio caro," Ricardo said as he put his arm around her and led her back to the car.

Lianne decided she did not want to go out to eat that evening, she was like a bottle of pop, constantly pacing up and down the apartment. Ricardo cooked but she just pushed the food around the plate. He was concerned because she had barely eaten anything at lunchtime, but he did not say anything to her.

At about 9:30 p.m., Ricardo's phone rang; he spoke in Italian for a few minutes and then the call ended. "Well?" Lianne asked, desperate to know what had been said.

"It was Francesco, he go to Alfonso on Sunday and will speak to him then if no one else there. But he also say Alfonso away next week on business so earliest he could meet would be the weekend."

Ricardo had obviously read Lianne's mind; she had been thinking of changing her return flight hoping that maybe she could see Alfonso on Monday, but that now seemed a waste of time. Ricardo continued, "Francesco will ring after he has spoken to Alfonso so we can do nothing now but wait."

Lianne was a little disappointed, after all the build-up over the last week or so, she had hoped things would move quickly. She sighed and then said, "I've waited for all these years, I'm sure I can wait another week."

Ricardo kissed her forehead tenderly and held her in his arms, "Si, another week."

Chapter 22

The rest of the weekend passed slowly. On the Saturday, Lianne and Ricardo went into Lucca to do some Christmas shopping, the shops were filled with wonderful food and the smells wafted down every walkway. Lianne was feeling hungry, having eaten little the day before, and so they stopped at one of the many cafe bars for a drink and a bite to eat.

"I think we need a list," Lianne said, taking some paper and a pen from her bag.

They drew up a list of everyone they needed to buy for and any ideas they had about what to get. As Lianne wrote down the names and ideas, she could not help but think back to Christmas the previous year, whilst her Mam was no longer able to eat and her speech was badly slurred, they had had a lovely day.

Lianne had bought her Mam a beautiful cashmere shawl, as she had felt the cold so much more towards the end. Margaret had felt very guilty about not having bought anything for Lianne for Christmas, but Lianne had just shrugged her shoulders and assured her Mam that she had everything she needed.

Lianne had put up a real tree in the lounge and there were decorations and lights everywhere, her Mam had always said there had been only a few decorations when she was growing up, which was why she had always gone overboard when Lianne was around.

They had spent most of the day sat in the lounge, Lianne had not bothered to cook just for herself and was happy just to be with her Mam. They watched the Queen on TV, the Sound of Music which had always been one of their favourites, and the repeats of Morecambe and Wise. As always, the sketch with Andre Previn had them laughing, but that laughter had turned to panic when Margaret had started choking.

Lianne immediately jumped into 'nurse' mode using the suction machine to help clear her chest as she had done so often in the past. And as often happened the whole episode had exhausted Margaret, and Lianne had left her to sleep for a couple of hours and had made herself something to eat. Beans on toast was not your usual Christmas fare, but Lianne did not care, she had little appetite anyway.

"Li…Lianne!" She looked up, suddenly conscious, that Ricardo was talking to her. "Ciao! You are with me again!"

"Sorry," she said, "just thinking. Right let's get this Christmas shopping done!" And with that they headed off.

By the time they returned to the apartment, much later that day, they were exhausted but had got presents for nearly everyone on their list, and Lianne had managed to buy Gemma a beautiful silk scarf and another for Diane—just to thank them both for supporting her, always.

They were both too tired to cook and so they headed to Giuseppe's, who was delighted to see them again. They ate pasta with a delicious salmon and cream sauce, which they mopped up with fresh bread; for dessert they had a homemade chocolate mousse, followed by coffee. By the time they got home, they were both yawning and fell asleep in each other's arms.

On the Sunday, they headed to Sofia's, who had offered to cook them lunch. As they sat around the table, Lianne told her what had happened with Francesco and that he was going to speak to her father that afternoon.

"You must be very…nervosa…nervous? But you must remember, this big shock for your papa, he need time to understand, you understand what I say?"

Lianne nodded, "I think so, and I know he may decide he doesn't want to see me or may even want a DNA test. I will just have to wait and see, but at least I will have done what my Mam wanted, and contacted him."

"Si, this very important."

With that, Sofia turned the conversation to Christmas and asked what their plans were. She explained that Isabella and Emilio had invited her over to their house and had asked her to ask them to join her. Ricardo took his lead from Lianne who thought it would be nice to spend the day with his family.

"I warn you," Sofia said, with a laugh, "those children are crazy!"

It was about 7:30 p.m. when Francesco finally telephoned; Lianne had just made them a sandwich before she started packing for her return flight the next day.

Ricardo was on the phone for quite some time and Lianne had no way of know what was being said—whether it was good news or bad. When the conversation finally finished, Lianne just sat staring at him.

"Is good news," Ricardo finally said. "Francesco say Alfonso very shocked and also sad that your Mama is gone. He does want to meet you…" before he could finish, Lianne was saying, "when, when?"

"He tell Francesco he need to speak to his children first…"

"Oh my God, I have siblings!"

"Per favore—let me finish! He speak them next weekend when he home and suggests he meet you, weekend after."

Part of her wanted to say that that was 2 weeks away, but the other part acknowledged that Alfonso would have to do this his way and if that meant waiting, then that was what she would have to do.

"That weekend, before Christmas," Ricardo continued, "when you are coming here anyway. This is I think good time, both Alfonso and his children have time to understand what is happening."

Lianne reluctantly agreed, another 2 weeks, she just had to wait another 2 weeks.

Chapter 23

On the Monday Lianne drove straight from the airport to Diane's, who was clearly surprised to see her.

"I'm sorry to turn up unannounced," Lianne said as Diane opened the door, "but I'm going to meet my dad, and I wanted to tell you first!"

"Oh, my goodness, I don't believe it! Come on in, I'll put the kettle on and you can tell me all about it!"

A few moments later, Lianne was sitting in the lounge and Diane had returned with 2 large mugs of tea and a packet of chocolate biscuits.

"This is a cause for celebration!" She said opening the packet. "So, tell me everything that has happened!"

Ten minutes later, Lianne had told Diane everything, about meeting with Francesco, waiting for the phone call, and then the final phone call when Francesco confirmed that Alfonso wanted to meet her.

"Apparently Alfonso's wife died last year, I don't know how or anything, so I suppose in some respects that makes things a little easier for him. And—" she suddenly exclaimed, "I've got siblings! I don't know how many or whether they're brothers or sisters, but it's definitely more than one!"

Diane said that she was really pleased and that she was certain that her Mam was 'up there' smiling.

"You just need to remember though love, that sometimes these reunions don't have happy endings. You may not get on with him, he may be totally different to the boy your Mam fell in love with; his children may resent you, especially as they haven't long lost their Mam. But on the other hand, that might help you bond—you'll have something in common. Just don't get your hopes up too soon, will you darling? I'd hate to see you get hurt."

Lianne completely understood, in fact Ricardo had said many of the same things the night before. "I know, I just hope and pray that it turns out OK." Lianne went on to explain that she was going to spend Christmas with Ricardo's family, which Diane thought was a good idea, but she promised that she would be over to see Diane again before she went.

"I will look forward to it," Diane said, as Lianne said her goodbyes and headed home.

The house looked really bare when she got home, there was no Christmas tree or decorations up, and so she vowed to do something about it the following day. She unpacked the few bits that she had brought back in her hand luggage and put a load in the washing machine before heading to the supermarket.

On her way, she decided to head to the crematorium; her Mam's ashes had been scattered, but there was still a plaque and Lianne liked to go there to 'talk to her'. She stopped to pick up some flowers and then headed over. It was a cold crisp day, but the sun was shining and the plaque glistened in the sunlight.

"Well, what do I say? I'm finally going to meet him Mam, I can't quite believe it. Everyone's warning me not to get my hopes up, but I can't imagine you ever falling in love with someone who isn't kind or considerate. It's going to be so strange finally meeting him."

"I wonder what would have happened if you'd told him about me when you'd first found out you were pregnant? We could have been living in Italy all these years, can you imagine! I think we'd probably both been the size of a house. Honestly Mam, the pasta all comes with thick creamy sauces and loads of bread!"

"Well, I'm going to go and do some food shopping now, but I'll be back to see you before Christmas Mam, night God bless."

Over the next few days, Lianne sorted out a load of stuff for work, put up some Christmas decorations and then made arrangements to speak to an agent about renting the house out, if she moved to Italy. She had initially thought that she would sell it but then decided that the safest option would be to rent. She also made arrangements to catch up with Gemma over the weekend and told her everything that had happened.

Gemma could not quite believe it. "Bloody hell Li, this is incredible. So basically, because I persuaded you to go to Italy for a long weekend, you are moving to Italy, have fallen in love with a sexy doctor, and found your dad!"

Lianne laughed, "Well if you put it like that, then yes, it's all down to you!"

"I just had a thought—I'll be able to come to Italy for some cheap holidays, maybe meet up with that sexy Marco guy again! There's only one problem—

who am I going to talk to when you're over there? I'll have to Face-Time you regularly, so you can help sort me out!"

The chat continued for a couple of hours during which they downed a few bottles of wine and put the world to right. When it was time to leave, both were a little emotional, each wondering what the future held for them. When it was time to go, Lianne gave Gemma the silk scarf and made her promise that she'd be over for a visit very soon.

The following day, Lianne went to see the estate agent to discuss her options with the house; there was no mortgage on it, so if she decided to sell, she would have a sizeable amount of money in the bank. The estate agent however agreed with Lianne that renting the property out, was the best option, at least in the short term.

He explained, that given the proximity to the university, she would have no problem renting it out and she could easily have four tenants in there, which would yield a good monthly income for her. Lianne could see the advantage of both and explained that she would like to take some time over the holiday period to think about things. In the meantime however, she arranged for the estate agent to visit the house and give her some figures.

Work had picked, as it always did, in the run up to Christmas. Whilst everyone was rushing around, buying thick woolly jumpers and long scarves. Lianne was already working on the company's promotions for the spring and summer fashions, which would be rolled out after the January sales.

There was the usual Christmas get together, and as she had not been the previous year, she wanted to make the effort this time. Everyone was meeting at a bar in the city centre, and then heading to a restaurant for a meal before the obligatory pub crawl.

She had chosen a forest green dress which she wore with black tights and ankle boots, the dress was one she had had for a number of years but had rarely worn and she did not really know why, until she got to the pub. Quite a few of the team had been drinking since they had finished work a couple of hours previously, and one of the lads, who usually would not say a word to anyone, piped up saying that she looked like a Christmas tree!

"Now I know why I don't wear it!" She said with a laugh.

They moved on to the restaurant and had the usual over-priced, poor-quality food. Lianne could not help being annoyed; she had eaten so much better in Italy for a lot less. After the meal, she made her excuses and left, whilst she was ecstatic at the prospect of meeting her dad, she was also very conscious that this was her first Christmas without her Mam.

Lianne made her way home, avoiding the throng of office workers who had all had far too much to drink. Everyone seemed so happy but she felt a whole mixture of things and did not really know whether to laugh or cry, but she knew she wanted to be on her own. She needed some time to process everything that had happened, and was about to happen.

She unlocked the front door and went upstairs to her Mam's bedroom, where there was an overwhelming sense of peace. She would often sit in her Mam's room and just think about everything that had happened; some people might feel uncomfortable about being in the room where someone close had taken their last breath, but she just remembered the happy times.

She remembered Christmas as a child; running into her Mam's room at some ridiculous hour and waking her up, because Father Christmas had been. She would unwrap all her presents and there would be paper everywhere but her Mam did not mind, she would show surprise at the doll or game that Father Christmas had brought and tell her she must have been a very good girl and was very lucky.

And Lianne was lucky, she knew that. She may not have had a father growing up, or siblings or grandparents, but she had everything she ever needed and no one could have loved her more. She was always amazed by friends in school who complained about their mums and dads who didn't listen to them or show any interest in their lives. Not so for Lianne, she talked to her Mam about anything and everything, and her Mam would always listen and offer advice if Lianne asked for it. She always had time for her and that was something Lianne would never forget.

Lianne's mind wandered, as she lay there, and quite soon, she fell into a deep sleep.

Chapter 24

In the final couple of days before she flew back to Italy, Lianne went to see Diane, as she promised she would. Diane loved the scarf and Lianne thanked her for all her support over the last year.

Diane knew that Christmas would have been a difficult time, even if Lianne wasn't meeting her dad and she made her promise that she would be kind to herself. "It's OK to have happy times you know, don't ever feel as if you're somehow being disloyal to your Mam because you're happy. But it's also equally important to take time out to be sad when you need to, it doesn't make you weak or ungrateful for all the wonderful things that are happening. It just makes you human. Don't forget that."

Lianne couldn't help but shed a tear or two. "It's all so crazy. Sometimes I feel I'm the luckiest person in the world and then I think I'm an orphan, with no family. I know I'm going to meet my dad, so I'm not an orphan but I don't know him, he doesn't know me. Does that make sense?"

"It makes perfect sense, he's your biological father, but he's not your dad yet, and he may never be. He may not feel able to accept you into his life now, this will all come as such a huge shock to him and he'll need to process everything, especially so soon after losing his wife. That's something that can only happen with time. So, you both need to take that time, take as much as you need—promise me that."

"I will, I promise."

After Lianne left Diane's, she headed back up to the crematorium to lay some fresh flowers and then she headed home to pack. Once she had, she decided to have a long soak and ran herself a nice bath; she lay there reading her kindle but gave up after a while. She must have read the same paragraph a dozen times and still had no idea what was happening, so she switched it off.

She closed her eyes and tried to imagine what her dad looked like; she had never thought that she looked much like her Mam so she must look like her father. Would she look like her siblings, she wondered. Would she even meet them? Her dad maybe meeting her to tell her to leave him and his family alone; he may not want anything to do with her.

So many questions.

The following day Lianne boarded her flight back to Italy, once again she had barely slept the night before and felt exhausted. She also felt quite sick with worry, having now convinced herself that her father wouldn't acknowledge her and that she would be on her own once again.

When she walked into the arrivals hall, Ricardo was waiting for her and was quite worried when he saw her, she looked pale and appeared to have lost weight since he'd seen her 2 weeks ago.

As usual, he swept her up in his arms and could feel that she had indeed lost weight.

"Mio caro, are you unwell? Was the flight bumpy?"

"I'm OK," she replied. "I just didn't sleep very well last night."

When they got in car and headed to Lucca, Lianne admitted that she was worried about meeting her father. Ricardo tried to reassure her but she was convinced now that her father wouldn't want a relationship with her and she would never meet her siblings. "If he wanted me in his life, I'm sure he wouldn't have waited 2 weeks to see me," she said, "and he won't want to tarnish his children's memories of their mother by admitting that he'd had a relationship with my Mam, even if it was years before he met his wife. So, I think this is going to be a fairly brief catch up."

Ricardo tried repeatedly to get her to consider an alternative scenario but she was having none of it, and so in the end he gave up trying.

Lianne didn't want to go out to eat that evening, so they ordered in pizza and sat quietly on the sofa. After they had eaten, Ricardo explained the plans he had made with Francesco; they would meet in a small cafe bar in Barga late on the Saturday morning, and Francesco would be there too. Lianne merely thanked Ricardo for making the arrangements and said no more.

"You very quiet Lianne, you not happy with plan?" He asked.

"I'm sorry," she replied, "I'm just really worried that he'll either want nothing to do with me or will be really disappointed. He might not like me! Anything could happen."

"You really are worrying too much. If your father not want you in life, then he tell Francesco he no meet you; so he want to see you. Si? And no one ever disappointed in you; you beautiful, funny, clever woman. I certain Alfonso love you like I do!" With a little more reassurance, Lianne finally started to come round but there was always that nagging feeling, that it would not be a fairy-tale ending.

They went to bed just after 11:00 p.m. and Ricardo fell asleep within minutes, with his arm wrapped around Lianne. She, on the other hand, was struggling to sleep, so she headed into the kitchen to get a drink. What Ricardo had said was logical, if Alfonso didn't want to see her, he would never have arranged to meet her. So why oh, why was her mind going round and round in circles as she imagined the many different ways that the whole idea of meeting her father could go wrong.

Lianne lay awake for several hours, mulling things over and finally fell asleep on the settee, which is where Ricardo found her when his alarm went off. He gently woke her and encouraged her to go to bed and try and get some more sleep, which she did.

When Lianne woke again, just before 10:00 a.m. she felt as if she'd been hit by a bus! Her eyes were stinging, and all in all she felt exhausted but she had things to do, so she climbed into the shower to try and wake herself up a bit. Once showered and dressed, she did some food shopping and went for a walk down by the river before heading back to the apartment. Ricardo could clearly see that she was struggling, and desperately wanted to take her mind off the meeting, but that was impossible. He did however, persuade her to go to Giuseppe's that evening, for a bite to eat.

Chapter 25

Lianne woke early on the Saturday, she tried to go back to sleep, but her mind was already whirring, so she eventually gave up and headed for the kitchen. She made a pot of coffee and sat at the table looking through some photographs that she had brought with her to show Alfonso, as well as the coral and silver bracelet he'd bought her Mam.

The photos made her smile; there was one of her when she was about 2 years old, on a battered old rocking horse; her dark hair was in pigtails and she was obviously loving every minute. There were very few photos of her with her Mam, especially when she was young, presumably, because her Mam was taking all the photos. There was a lovely one of them both on the beach on what must have been a beautiful summers day. Lianne vaguely remembered going there with her Mam and Diane. There was another from her prom night after her A levels. She was in a gold halter neck dress that her Mam had made for her, and they had quickly got someone to take a photo of them together before she joined her friends in the limo they had hired.

Happy times.

Lianne and Ricardo left his apartment just after 10:00 a.m. Lianne had eventually decided to wear a baby-blue, faux cashmere jumper, with a pair of dark denim jeans. She wore a pair of blue suede ankle boots and had a thick jacket, as well as a hat and gloves, as Ricardo had warned her that it would be a lot colder up in the mountains.

When they got to Barga, things looked vaguely familiar and Lianne remembered her visit earlier in the year with Gemma, and how they had walked up to the old church on the top of the hill. Ricardo was able to park the car a few minutes' walk from the cafe where they were due to meet, and Lianne quickly realised it was the same cafe where she'd sat with Gemma. Ricardo held Lianne's hand as they walked toward the cafe and he could feel her physically shaking as they got nearer to their destination. It was clear that she was absolutely terrified of what might happen in the next couple of hours, when they would meet Francesco and Alfonso.

As they stepped through the door into the warm, cosy cafe Lianne immediately saw Francesco sitting at a table in the corner, with another man. He looked at her and obviously said something to his companion, as he turned around and looked straight at her. Ricardo held her hand even tighter as they walked over.

Lianne smiled at Francesco and turned to look directly at her father. Lianne recognised him immediately from her Mam's photos, he was tall and slim, with dark hair speckled with the occasional grey, and dark brown eyes just like hers. And for a split second they looked directly at each other and there were tears running down Alfonso's cheeks; Alfonso put his arms around her and held her close, as the tears ran down her face too. For what seemed like forever, they just stood there holding each other, and all of Lianne's fears evaporated; she knew she'd found her dad, not just her biological father.

They all sat around the table and Alfonso held Lianne's hand; they ordered drinks and Lianne introduced Ricardo to Alfonso.

"I cannot believe how like Maggie you are," Alfonso said, "you look just like she did when I meet her. I so sorry to hear she is gone; she was very beautiful woman and I loved her very much. Francesco say to me you not know about me until Maggie has gone, Si?"

"That's right. Mam knew she was very ill, but had plenty of time to dispose of your letters if she had wanted to, so she must have wanted me to find them and so find you."

"You must believe, I know nothing about you until Francesco tell me 2 weeks ago. If I had I would have been there."

"It's OK, I know you didn't know anything about me. From what my aunt told me, my Mam didn't want you to feel obligated to her or me because of a holiday romance, she was worried that you wouldn't be able to pursue your dreams."

"Did your Mam ever marry?" Francesco asked.

"No," Lianne replied. "I don't think she ever had a boyfriend either. I certainly don't remember her going out on a date or bringing someone home. From what my aunt said, she never stopped loving you, Alfonso."

"And I always love her, she was my first love," he said with a tear in his eye.

The waitress brought their drinks as they continued to talk, Alfonso wanted to know all about Lianne, her life and about Maggie. He explained that he had been devastated when Maggie stopped answering his letters, he had even thought of flying to Cardiff to try and find her, but his parents had been dead set against any such trip. His friends, including Gino, had spent weeks trying to convince him that she was not worthy of his love and that she had obviously just used him; in the end, when there was still no letter, he started to believe it too.

Alfonso had gone to university as planned to do his degree in architecture, and in his final year, he had met Greta, they dated for several years before finally getting married. They had had three children—two girls and a boy—Mia, Gabriella, and Lorenzo. They were 21, 16 and 18 respectively.

"So," Alfonso said, "you have a brother and two sisters." Alfonso went on to say that Greta had always known about Maggie, he had always been very honest with her and she had known that Maggie always was and always would be his first love. But they had had a good life together and he had made sure that he committed himself to her and their children.

"I can't quite believe that I have siblings, I've always been an only child and never expected that to change."

"I have told them about you," Alfonso said in response to Lianne's unspoken question. "Obviously they very shocked, but they are OK. I think they worry that I unfaithful to Greta, but I promise them I meet their mother many years after I see Maggie. They know I see you today and they say they want meet you too."

"Wow that would be amazing, I can't wait. Do you have photos of them?" Lianne asked. Alfonso produced half a dozen photos of his wife and his 3 children and Lianne was fascinated to see them. She could even see similarities between herself and one of his daughters.

Lianne showed Alfonso the photos she had brought from home, as well as the letters and the bracelet. Alfonso smiled when he saw the latter and told Lianne the story of how he had saved his money from his job in the ice-cream parlour in order to buy the bracelet for Maggie as a going away present.

Alfonso went on to say that he would like Lianne to meet her siblings in Bologna where he lived, if that was possible, and he appreciated that it was a long drive from Lucca.

"This not a problem," Ricardo said. "I can drive Lianne to Bologna anytime."

Alfonso was delighted, he was conscious that his family would feel happier doing it at home, in fact they had insisted when he had told them about Lianne.

Things had not been quite as straightforward as he was leading Lianne to believe. They had all been very suspicious about Lianne—was he positive she was his daughter; was he going to get a DNA test; did their mum know about Lianne? They had bombarded him with questions, most of which he could not answer, as he had not known that Lianne existed until a few days before he had told them. He really hoped that when they met Lianne, their fears would evaporate.

It was agreed that Lianne and Ricardo would travel to Bologna the day after Boxing Day, and on the drive back to Lucca Lianne was like a bottle of pop. She was so excited, the meeting with her father had gone better than she had hoped and she could not wait now to see him again and to meet her siblings.

Chapter 26

There were still a few days until Christmas, and Lianne decided that she wanted to buy her father and siblings small presents to give them when they met. The following day, when Ricardo went to the surgery, she headed into Lucca to try and find gifts for them all. She walked around the shops for hours but got absolutely nowhere and returned to the apartment with nothing.

"I don't know what to do," she told Ricardo that evening. "I think the problem is that I just don't know them, so I have no idea what they would like or dislike."

"Si, this is true. Why you not make something for them, not buy presents?"

"Like what?"

"Can you make something to eat that we can take with us? Something from home?"

"That's not a bad idea," she replied, "we have a Welsh cake called Bara Brith, and small cakes called Welsh cakes! I could make a load to take over! You're a genius," she added kissing his cheek, "now all I need are recipes!"

The following day, Lianne emailed Diane asking her for recipes and then she made a list of all the shopping she needed before heading out.

Lianne wandered around the shops picking up all the ingredients she needed, she couldn't help but be struck by the difference between Christmas in Lucca and Christmas back home. There were certainly plenty of lights adorning the shops and public buildings, just as there would be at home, but if you closed your eyes the 'smell' of Christmas was different. There were so many different aromas bombarding her senses, some familiar some not. The voices were different—no Welsh accents; she was beginning to pick up a few Italian words, but most of the time she had no idea what people were saying.

Lianne found a little Pasticceria, a shop selling cakes and pastries. It was cold, certainly, but the sun was shining, so she sat at one of several small tables outside and enjoyed a pastry with her coffee. The pastry was delicious with warming spices and dried fruit; she enjoyed every morsel, as she sat watching the world go by. Lianne had always been a 'people watcher'—she was fascinated by the way people dressed, the way they walked and talked. The media was full of images of 'perfect' people that resulted in so many youngsters, in particular, feeling that they were just not good enough. But nobody was perfect, nobody at all, and so it was impossible to achieve perfection. Far better to be yourself, be an individual; and as Lianne sat drinking her coffee, there were certainly some interesting individuals in Lucca.

There was the well-dressed older lady tottering around in high heeled shoes, with a sandy coloured chihuahua popping its head out of a large Louis Vuitton bag. The teenager wearing flip flops, shorts and a t-shirt with a bobble hat on his head, who looked as if he didn't quite know what season it was! A little old lady who was almost invisible in the crowd; dressed all in black and hunched over, she moved purposefully through the Christmas shoppers, determined not to let them get in the way. And there was the middle-aged man, staring into the jewellery shop window, wondering what on earth he could buy his wife/girlfriend (or both!) which would look as if he'd put some real thought into his gift. Lianne smiled, such a mish mash of different people, all with their own stories to tell, just like her.

Lianne finished her coffee and left a small tip on the table before heading back into the throng of shoppers. She decided to head back to the apartment and to make a start on wrapping Christmas presents, it would be easier to do without Ricardo there.

Ricardo arrived home just after 6:00 p.m., to find Lianne in a sea of wrapping paper and sellotape! "You be very busy," he said, "so many presents for me! I very happy!"

"Don't be so cheeky!" She said with a laugh. "You may get one present, if you are on Santa's good list!"

"I always good," he said with a cheeky grin, kissing the top of her head. "I go shower, then we eat? It smell very good!"

Lianne had made a chicken casserole with fresh veg and mashed potatoes, which was ready when he emerged from the bedroom 20 minutes later, in a t-shirt and joggers. Lianne dished up and as always, they chatted as they ate about the kind of day they'd had. Lianne didn't have much to say, but she told Ricardo about her shopping trip and some of the people she'd seen.

Ricardo had been with his patients all day and amongst the usual coughs and colds there had been some 'good' patients—a middle aged couple who had tried for many years for a baby and finally conceived through IVF and the wife was 12 weeks pregnant; and then there was the teenage boy who had been waiting for a kidney transplant, and who had finally had 'the call' which hopefully would signal a whole new life for him.

After they had eaten, they sat quietly on the settee, Ricardo was reading some medical paper and Lianne was enjoying her book. They shared a bottle of wine and were quite content to just be in each other's company; no need to make conversation.

The next day was Christmas Eve, Ricardo wasn't working, but he was on call so they couldn't stray too far, but they did go for a walk and enjoyed a coffee at a local cafe bar. Ricardo was only called out once and Lianne used that time to sort out some bits and pieces.

Lianne woke just after 8:00 a.m. on Christmas Day, Ricardo was already awake and he was sat up in bed watching her. He smiled as she opened her eyes and kissed her forehead.

"Merry Christmas Lianne," he said softly, as she stretched and rolled over to cuddle into him and they lay there for a few minutes, before Ricardo felt a small teardrop run down her cheek and on to his chest.

"Are you OK il mio amore? This must be difficult day for you without your Mama, for first time."

"It is, Christmas was so strange last year and I knew I'd never have another Christmas with Mam. I think I thought time would stop when she passed but of course it didn't and here I am having embarked on a whole new chapter in my life. And I'm happy but I feel guilty for being happy, does that make sense?"

"I think it normal to feel like you do. This very unusual time and so much happened since last Christmas."

"It certainly has," Lianne said, as she lifted her head up and kissed him very softly on the lips. "But I have you and that's all that matters." They kissed again, this time more ardently, and it was an hour later, when they realised the time.

Lianne was conscious that Isabella was cooking them lunch and she didn't want to be late, it would be disrespectful, but Ricardo kept dragging her back into bed despite her protests.

Reluctantly he let her go eventually, and she jumped into the shower.

An hour later, she was ready. She wore a plum-coloured dress that she had treated herself to, with black tights and black ankle boots. She'd styled her long, dark, hair and had applied just enough make up to enhance her features; she looked absolutely stunning and Ricardo felt he was the luckiest man in the world.

When they arrived at Isabella's, Lianne was glad she'd made an effort, it was clear the family 'dressed' for Christmas Day. Sofia had already arrived and she was playing with the children, whilst Isabella was in the kitchen. The smells that wafted into lounge were amazing. Lianne was excited to try her first Italian Christmas meal and said as much to Sofia and Isabella, as she offered to help.

Half an hour later, Isabella brought a platter of antipasto to the table and invited everyone to sit down. There were various cured meats on offer, as well as cheeses and olives; a little while later she brought out some stuffed pasta which they all tucked into. It was absolutely delicious and Lianne thoroughly enjoyed it.

"That was incredible, thank you," she said and with that, Sofia and Isabella started laughing "I don't understand, have I done something wrong?"

"No, no no," Ricardo said, smiling, "we not have main course yet! There plenty more to come!"

"More! I'll explode!" And they all laughed!

There was a sense of relief when Lianne realised that the Christmas lunch would be served over a period of 3 or 4 hours, so she'd have plenty of time to let her food go down. Sometime later, Isabella brought in the main course; braised beef with a red wine jus and a selection of vegetables. As she expected, the beef was delicious and it wasn't long before everyone had cleared their plates and were sitting back in their chairs praising Isabella on cooking a fabulous Christmas dinner. By this time the children were getting impatient and desperately wanted to unwrap their presents, so everyone retired to the lounge with Isabella telling everyone that they would have dessert later.

The presents were handed out, and Lianne was amazed to find that Ricardo's family had bought her presents too; she hadn't expected it. The Christmas she was with Grant, his parents never gave her anything. They seemed to think that Lianne had chased after him and was only interested in his family's money. Nothing could have been further from the truth.

Once all the presents had been handed out, they took it in turns to open their gifts. Sofia had bought Lianne a beautiful cashmere jumper in baby-pink, which she loved; Isabella and Emilio gave her a lovely pair of earrings which were just the sort of thing that Lianne would wear. Then Ricardo gave her his present, it was a beautiful cream leather handbag and Lianne recognised it as the one she had seen in a shop in Lucca when she had been out with Ricardo a few weeks beforehand. She knew it had cost more than 300€ which was more money than she'd ever consider spending on a bag, but it was absolutely gorgeous and she thanked Ricardo profusely.

"I glad you like the bag," he said.

"I don't just like it, I love it!" She replied. "It's absolutely gorgeous but you really shouldn't have spent all that money on me."

"Ti amo, moltissimo. I am loving you very much and I want you to have the best of things."

"Well thank you, it is the most beautiful bag I have ever seen."

Finally, it was Ricardo's turn to open his presents; Lianne had bought him an Apple Watch, which he had been saying he wanted for some time. She had also bought him a navy Ralph Lauren polo shirt, which she knew would look good on him.

Once everyone had opened all their presents, Isabella disappeared into the kitchen, emerging a little while later with dessert—caggionetti. Lianne had never come across it before, it was a stuffed pasta, but this time filled with sweet fruits, nuts and honey, and it was delicious served warm with a vanilla sauce.

By the time dessert was finished, everyone was sat around the living room feeling as if they were going to explode, they had all eaten so much! The children were beginning to fall asleep and so Isabella got them changed into their pyjamas and tucked them up in bed. It was nearly 8:30 p.m. and Ricardo and Lianne decided to head back to the apartment, as Lianne wanted to be up early the next day to start baking for her meeting with Alfonso and her siblings.

They thanked Isabella profusely for the wonderful food and the excellent company. It had been a completely different Christmas Day for Lianne, and was probably just what she needed. As they went to leave, Lianne hugged Sofia and thanked her for making Christmas so special and then said it in Italian; she'd been practicing!

"Grazie mille per aver reso questo Natale cosi speciale."

"Splendid!" She replied. "And I hope this one of many Christmas' with our family."

"Grazie."

They drove home quietly, Lianne lost in her thoughts and Ricardo not wanting to interrupt; he knew it was important for her to have some down time and to reflect on the previous year.

Once back in the apartment, they both changed into comfortable joggers and t-shirts before snuggling up on the settee with a bottle of wine. Neither had drunk much during the day, so it was nice to relax with a glass of wine once they were home. However, Ricardo seemed to be struggling to relax and kept shifting position, as if trying to get comfortable.

"Are you OK?" Lianne asked.

"Si, si," came the reply, but he carried on sighing and moving around.

"What on Earth is the matter? Can't you keep still? Anyone would think you had ants in your pants!" Ricardo gave her a very quizzical expression. "It's OK, it's just a saying when someone can't keep still!" She reassured him.

"Mi scusi." Ricardo said before disappearing into the bedroom. He returned a few moments later and sat next to Lianne. "I have more present for you, but not sure if I upset you if I give it."

"Why would it upset me?" Lianne said. "Unless it's a flight back to Cardiff!"

With that, Ricardo slid off the settee on to his knees and produced a small, cream leather box from his pocket. Lianne suddenly realised what was happening and gasped.

"Lianne, I am loving you very much. We not know each other very long but I am knowing that I want to stay here and grow old with you. Will you marry me?"

The tears were pouring down Lianne's cheeks and for a moment Ricardo thought he'd done the wrong thing, but then Lianne blubbered, "Yes, yes, yes!" She flung her arms around him and smothered him in kisses and tears. He slipped the beautiful diamond and platinum ring on to her finger and they held each other tight for what seemed like an eternity.

As they slipped into bed later that evening, Lianne was overwhelmed by everything that had happened and thanked him for a truly wonderful Christmas in the best way she knew.

Chapter 27

They woke to a beautiful clear morning, again it was chilly outside but the sun was shining and everything seemed to sparkle, especially the diamond on Lianne's left hand. After breakfast, Lianne started baking and the kitchen was filled with the aroma of Bara Brith and Welsh cakes. Ricardo tried a few of the latter, whilst they were still warm, and declared that as his wife, he would expect Lianne to bake them every week as they were delicious! Lianne laughed and promised to be a good wife, who would obey!

After she'd finished baking, Lianne went and showered before putting on a little make up and getting dressed. She'd told Ricardo that she was going to FaceTime Diane and Gemma to tell them the good news and wanted to look her best.

She tried Diane first, who answered within a couple of rings. Diane was delighted to see her and asked how her Christmas had been; Lianne told her all about the wonderful day they had spent at Isabella's and the incredible food they'd eaten.

"It sounds as if it was just what you needed," Diane said. "I'm so glad you were able to enjoy yourself, I was worried."

"No need to worry, it was a lovely day. Obviously, I thought a lot about Mam, but I think she'd be happy that I'm happy, if you know what I mean! There was something else as well that made the day extra special…" and with that Lianne held her left hand up to the camera and Diane shrieked!

"Oh, my goodness! I'm so happy for you Lianne, you deserve this!"

"I'm over the moon! Ricardo is really a terrific guy and he makes me very happy. And," she added a little giggle, "the irony's not lost on me; I came to Italy because my Mam fell in love with an Italian boy and now I've done the same!" They both laughed.

Lianne and Diane continued chatting for another 10 minutes and when they said goodbye, Lianne promised she'd let Diane know how the meeting with her siblings went the next day.

Lianne then had another long chat with Gemma who shrieked with delight at the sight of the engagement ring, and then asked if Marco would be at the wedding!

Once she'd finished talking to Gemma, Ricardo said he wanted to tell his Mama about the engagement and they both Face-Timed her. Sofia was absolutely delighted for the two of them and she said she couldn't have asked for a lovelier daughter-in-law.

"When you get married?" She asked "You have a day?"

"Not yet," Lianne answered with a laugh, "we haven't talked about any of that stuff yet."

"Si, si. You have big day tomorrow meeting your family, there lot of time to plan wedding after."

They chatted a little longer and then Lianne left Ricardo to carry on talking to his Mama in Italian, as she didn't expect her to speak English the whole time. She had already decided that she was going to learn to speak Italian properly in the new year, after all, if she was going to be Ricardo's wife she'd need to live and work in Italy, and that meant learning the language. Actually, there were a lot of things she needed to do, so picking up a paper and pen she sat at the small table and started writing her list.

Call estate agent—sell or rent house?

What do I do with furniture, etc if I sell?

Move belongings to Italy? Is there enough room in the flat?

Speak to work, can I work remotely and just fly back when absolutely necessary?

Lianne was still working on her list when Ricardo finished talking to Sofia.

"Mama very happy that we marry," he said, "she say you are very beautiful woman outside and in."

"I'm very happy too. I can't believe everything that's happened this year. Last Christmas was difficult and I knew Mam wouldn't be with me much longer, but since she's gone, I have a whole new family with you and I have found my dad, something I never thought I'd do. I'd give anything to have Mam back, I miss her so much and that will never stop, but I have a new life now with you."

The rest of the day was spent quietly, but as time went on Lianne started to get more anxious at the prospect of meeting her siblings. Ricardo tried to reassure her that everything would be alright, just as it had been when she met her father, but nothing really helped, and in the end, he just accepted that this was how Lianne was, and left her to her thoughts.

Lianne had another restless night and was awake early, Ricardo found her wrapped in a blanket drinking coffee on the balcony, when he got up a little later.

"You no sleep good, will be very tired later."

"I know," she replied. "I'm just very worried about how things will be today. What if they hate me, or hate my Mam? They may not like me becoming a part of Alfonso's life, especially so soon after losing their Mam too. Maybe I should just cancel…"

As she uttered those words, her phone pinged to indicate that she had a text message; it was Alfonso just wanting to let her know that he was looking forward to seeing her later that morning. It immediately brought a smile to her face and Ricardo was better able to calm her down. He suggested she go and shower whilst he made breakfast; she thanked him for putting up with her and her anxiety.

"You very hard to live with!" He said with a smile on his face "now go and shower while I make breakfast!"

"Thank you!"

Lianne disappeared into bedroom and emerged 15 minutes later, with her hair still wrapped in a towel. Breakfast was ready, as Ricardo had promised, and he was pleased to see that she was actually eating.

"We leave here in one hour," he said, when they had finished eating, "so we have plenty time to get to Bologna."

"I will be ready," she promised before disappearing off into the bedroom again. She had laid out her clothes—a pair of slim fitting black trousers, which she was going to wear with the beautiful jumper Sofia had bought her. But first of all, she dried her hair off and then set about applying her makeup, going for a very natural look that enhanced her appearance but tried to hide the dark circles under her eyes from another night of tossing and turning. Eventually, she was ready; she put her bits and pieces into her bag and packed up the Bara Brith and Welsh cakes that she had made for them.

Ricardo told her how beautiful she looked and then carried the stuff to the car. Once it was loaded, they set off toward Bologna. It would take about an hour to get there, and Lianne sat in silence most of the way.

They found the address fairly easily; it was a fairly modern 2-storey house on the outskirts of Bologna. There was an 'in and out' driveway and Ricardo pulled in behind two other cars. Alfonso appeared at the doorway, he shook Ricardo's hand and embraced Lianne, kissing both her cheeks. Lianne smiled at him and she could see the familiarity in his eyes, he too was smiling as he showed them into a large hallway, with a central staircase. On the right-hand side, there were double doors that were open and Lianne could see a beautiful old dining table and a dresser covered in numerous photo frames. Alfonso guided them through the double doors on the left which opened into a large lounge, that extended all the way to the back of the house. There were a number of settees and chairs, some which were occupied.

"Lianne, these my children—Mia, her friend Enrico, my son Lorenzo, and youngest daughter Gabriella." Then looking at his children he said, "and this is your big sister Lianne."

There were a few muttered "ciao's" and it was clear to Lianne that the three of them were rather wary of this intruder who claimed be their father's child.

"Mi fa molto piacere conoscerti." Lianne had been practicing, "I am very pleased to meet you," she said.

Alfonso then introduced Ricardo who greeted them in Italian and they responded in Italian. He invited Lianne and Ricardo to sit down and brought in a pot of coffee as well as soft drinks. As he served the drinks Lianne produced the boxes from her bag and opened them showing her siblings what she had made. Ricardo then explained in Italian that the cakes were a gift from Lianne, that they were traditional cakes from Wales where she was from, and that she had made them especially for them.

Lorenzo being a typical teenage boy was always hungry, and so he was the first to try Lianne's offerings.

"Mmm, molto bella," he said. Which was obviously a good endorsement and the others helped themselves too. Everyone seemed to enjoy the cakes and it wasn't long before all that remained in the boxes were crumbs.

When everyone had finished eating, Lianne asked Ricardo if he would translate what she was about to say, which he agreed.

"I was very sorry to hear about you mother, I lost my Mam earlier this year, so I know how hard it is," they each nodded. "I want you to know that I knew nothing about my father until after my Mam died, only then did I find the letters they had sent to each other as teenagers. I wanted to try and find my father, but

I have never wanted to…take him from you or get in the way. If he had said he wanted nothing to do with me, I would have walked away. I wouldn't have been happy, but I would have respected his decision. If you don't want me to be a part of your family, I will respect that too. But it is important that you know that what happened between my Mam and your father was many years before he met your mother, and your father never knew I existed until a couple of months ago."

There were a few murmurings and it was Mia who spoke first and she asked her father to translate; when she had finished speaking, Alfonso spoke back to her.

"Mia asks if I have a DNA test to prove you mine, I tell her this not necessary."

"I am very happy to agree to a test if that's what you and your children want, I have nothing to hide and no reason to doubt what I've been told."

"I think you my sister," Gabriella said with a smile "we are looking same like Babbo!" Lianne too had noticed the similarity between herself and Gabriella, not Mia so much who presumably looked more like her Mam.

"I very sorry you look like me!" Alfonso said jokingly.

After a few awkward minutes, that seemed like hours, the three siblings started to open up a bit and the conversation began to flow. It was clear that Mia and Lorenzo spoke little English but Gabriella had studied it in school and intended to continue, as she hoped to work in the tourism industry.

Lianne explained about her life in Cardiff and her work; she told them about her Mam and what had happened, how she had found the letters in a box at the back of the wardrobe and how that had led her to Lucca. She told them about how she had met Ricardo, and they laughed at the story of Gemma in her ridiculous shoes.

"And I intend to move to Italy now and work from here, as Ricardo has asked me to marry him!" And with that she showed them the diamond ring on her finger.

"Magnificent!" Alfonso exclaimed, "this very good news!" With that he disappeared and returned a few minutes later with some sparkling wine and glasses.

After they had all congratulated Lianne and Ricardo, Mia spoke:

"I sorry your Mama gone, it very sad for me to lose Mama and you too. But it good you find Babbo." Lianne knew this was a big step forward, and the sisters hugged. Gabriella joined in too and the three girls smiled at each other. Lorenzo didn't say very much other than wanting to know if Lianne could make some more cakes!

The rest of the afternoon went well, Alfonso had prepared an array of cold meats and cheeses for them to eat with fresh bread, and the conversation flowed more easily now that the ice had been broken. Lianne produced a load of photos of herself and her Mam and her resemblance to Gabriella when she was younger, was quite startling. The girls asked about her wedding and she explained that they hadn't had a chance to make any plans but she hoped they wouldn't have to wait too long.

Lianne was sorry when it was time to leave, but she didn't want to outstay her welcome and Ricardo needed to get back, as he had work the next day. They all hugged as they said goodbye and agreed that they would meet again soon. As they drove home Lianne was beaming and couldn't stop talking about her brother and sisters; it was such a relief that things had gone well. She wasn't naive to think that one visit meant that she was now a part of the family, but it had been a good start. After about 20 minutes of non-stop talking, Lianne suddenly announced that she was tired and Ricardo laughed.

"I wonder why this is?" He said, and they both laughed.

Chapter 28

The next few days were spent quietly, Ricardo was working and Lianne was going through her work emails and putting together a report which she hoped would enable her to work remotely from Lucca and just travel back to the UK when necessary. She emphasised the advantages of being in Italy and the opportunities this presented to expand the company's horizons, and to take on-board Italian concepts of fashion for both men and women.

Once she had finished writing her report, she made a start on sorting her personal life out; in many respects it made sense to sell her Mam's house and to use that capital to buy a bigger place in Lucca. Ricardo's apartment was lovely and it was only a 10 minutes' drive from his surgery, but it was only one bedroom and if she was going to move to Lucca permanently, she would like to have more space. She wanted children, and it would be nice to have some outside space for them to play in, so a bigger house would be ideal.

However, she was conscious that the estate agent had encouraged her to rent the house out; it was conveniently situated near the university and there was always a market for student accommodation. The agent had indicated that if it was marketed for 4 students, the income would be around £2,000 a month. Which would make a huge difference and could pay for a mortgage on a new property in Lucca. So, there were clear advantages, but Lianne could also see some disadvantages; in many ways she felt uncomfortable at the thought of students in her Mam's house, they weren't renowned for taking care of property and there would inevitably be damage. She knew that if she sold it, a buyer would probably rent it out anyway, but at least it wouldn't be her Mam's house anymore, if that made any sense.

There was a lot to think about and she really needed to know what Ricardo's thoughts were; they hadn't even discussed whether or not they wanted children, so there was no point in jumping the gun.

That evening, when Ricardo came home Lianne had cooked a lamb stew, it was one of those meals that always reminded her of her childhood. Her Mam would often make a large pot of stew which would last them a couple of days; she'd use the cheaper cuts of meat and add loads of vegetables and pulses.

"Something smell very good," Ricardo said, as he walked through the door. "I very hungry as no time for lunch today."

"It'll be ready in a few minutes," Lianne replied and Ricardo disappeared into the bedroom to change out of his suit. When he returned, the stew was on the table along with some fresh bread and a bottle of red wine.

The stew hardly touched the sides and Ricardo mopped up every last drop with bread. "Mmm. I know there good reason why I ask you to marry me. This very good!"

Lianne laughed as she cleared away the plates and then joined Ricardo on the settee. They talked for a few minutes about his day and then she changed the subject to the house.

"I need to decide what I'm going to do with my Mam's house," she said, "and a lot depends on what we're going to do."

"OK," Ricardo said, not really knowing where the conversation was heading. "You tell me what you are thinking."

"Ok here goes. Do you want to have children?"

"Si. Not now, but yes when we married, I want to have bambini. Is this not what you want?"

"I definitely want to have children, at least two, maybe three." Ricardo nodded as if to say that was what he was thinking too. "I need to decide what to do with the house in Cardiff," Lianne continued. "If we're going to have children, we need a bigger place and the money from the house would enable us to buy somewhere plenty big enough."

"I thought they tell you no sell, but rent. Is this not so?"

"It is, but I'm not sure I can cope with the idea of someone else in my house. Do you understand?" Ricardo nodded. "The house is full of memories; I don't want to tarnish those by having students in the house, wrecking everything."

"Si. I understand this. If you sell you break all—how you say—chains with house."

"Break my links to the house," Lianne said. "It wouldn't be mine anymore and I would never have to go back to the house, I'd just keep my memories."

"I understand, but you no have to sell if you not want to. We can still buy bigger place for the bambinos!"

"I'll have another think about it, but I think I want to sell."

New Year's Eve was spent quietly; Ricardo and Lianne went for long walk in the afternoon and took the opportunity to look in some estate agent windows, to find out what was on the market.

There wasn't much available but both felt certain there would be more around in the next couple of months.

In the evening, they went out for something to eat and then watched the fireworks from the balcony at midnight. They kept things quiet and low key; Lianne in particular felt that whilst the New Year meant a new life with Ricardo, it also meant saying goodbye again to her Mam.

Last New Year's Eve had been so strange, Lianne had known that her Mam didn't have much longer and so the New Year then meant a step closer to losing her. She hadn't even stayed up to see the New Year in last year; her Mam had fallen asleep just after 9:00 p.m. and so Lianne had headed to bed shortly after, best to take the opportunity to sleep whilst she could. As it was; she'd been woken at about 2:00 a.m. by her Mam's alarm, and it had taken some time to settle her, so she was glad for the sleep she had had.

When Ricardo and Lianne climbed into bed shortly before 1:00 a.m., she had cuddled into him and he held her tight whilst she quietly sobbed. He didn't say anything, there was no need, he just cradled her until she finally fell asleep.

The following day, they had been invited to Sofia's for lunch, it was the first time they had seen her properly since Christmas Day. Sofia had wanted it to be a bit of a celebration of their engagement, but had respected Lianne's wishes to keep it low key.

When they arrived at the house, the aroma of homemade lasagne wafted through the air and Sofia enveloped Lianne in arms and held her tight calling her, her 'new daughter'!

Sofia poured them both a glass of wine and said that lunch would be ready in about 30 minutes. "So, tell me what happens when you meet your family? Are they welcoming you?"

Lianne explained that they had been somewhat reserved at first and that Mia had even suggested that she should take a DNA test but her father had said that wasn't necessary.

"Gabriella was more chatty," she continued, "and to be honest we look very similar. So I don't think there's any doubt who my father is! But I know it's going to take time for them to trust and accept me, so I'll just have to be patient."

"They very lucky to have such a good person for a sister," Sofia added before heading to the kitchen.

As always, the meal was excellent, and afterwards Sofia wanted to know if they had made any plans for the wedding, she was obviously very excited about it all.

"We no make plans yet," Ricardo said, "but we will look for bigger house, so we have much room for the bambini's!"

Sofia looked at him and her jaw dropped. "No, no Mama! No bambini now, but we want when we are married and we need bigger house!"

They all laughed and continued to chat generally about moving house and the wedding. Lianne said she would want to keep the wedding fairly small, but that she'd like to get married in a church in Italy if possible. There were only a few people she would want to invite from back home. Such as, Diane and Gemma, and then it would just be her new Italian family. Ricardo agreed that other than a few close friends, he would only be looking at inviting his immediate family so numbers would be small.

"I even think," he said, "that if we buy house with good outside room, we could have celebrating there."

"I love that idea," Lianne said, "it would make it more personal, more special!"

"I think we need to find house then!"

A few days later, Lianne headed back to Cardiff. It felt really strange, it was her home, where she'd grown up, but it didn't feel the same any more. Her home was in Lucca now with Ricardo. The house was cold when she arrived, which made it feel even less like home. She soon worked out that the water pressure had dropped which was why the boiler hadn't kicked in; the house warmed up fairly quickly after she'd topped up the water.

Lianne emptied the small bag of groceries, she'd picked up on her way back from the airport; nothing much just some milk, bread, cereal, etc. She put the kettle on and whilst she waited for the water to boil, she made a start sorting out the mail. Most of it was rubbish—the usual junk mail—but there were also a few Christmas cards, and her credit card statement. Having made a cup of tea, she worked her way through it and was surprised to find a letter addressed to her Mam.

She held it in her hand for a few moments before opening it up. She should have realised that it wasn't anything important, as she'd notified everyone who needed to know of her Mam's passing; it was just the usual junk mail. This time, advising that a local department store was going to be having its 'best ever sale'. It was nonsense that she could just put into the recycling bin, but there was that awful feeling in the pit of her stomach that there were other companies out there who would carry on sending through the junk mail because they didn't know what had happened, and to be honest Lianne didn't see why she needed to tell them. She decided that in future she would mark all future junk mail "return to sender". Hopefully they would get the message.

Lianne drank her cup of tea and then rang the estate agent to advise him that she intended to sell the house rather than rent it out. He did his best to try and convince her to reconsider, but her mind was made up. It was agreed that he would call at the weekend to take some photos and measurements so that they could advertise the house sale. Lianne was not naive, she knew the house needed modernising and the price would reflect that, but she saw little point in trying to get the work done herself. Anyone buying it, was bound to make changes and she really didn't the hassle of trying to coordinate work from Lucca.

Lianne quickly sent texts to Diane and Gemma to let them know she was home, before popping her few bits and pieces in the washing machine.

Chapter 29

Lianne went into work the following day, and had a meeting with her boss, Helen, to discuss her move to Italy. Both felt really confident that the physical distance between them wouldn't cause any problems, so much was done by email and the use of things like, Face-Time, Teams and Zoom, meant that Lianne could easily be present—albeit virtually—for any meetings that she needed to be at. And of course, it was only a 2-hour flight and fares were relatively cheap, so she could always fly over, if she really needed to.

"I also agree with you that there could be some real advantages to having you in Italy," Helen said. "It would give us real opportunities to source Italian suppliers and provide our customers with something a bit different. Italian fashion has always had an edge to it and I think people would like that."

Lianne agreed, she'd looked into the whole idea of sourcing Italian suppliers when she'd put together her request, and she knew there could be real scope to bring Italian fashion into the store, which could give them an edge over their competitors.

Helen asked when Lianne would be moving and Lianne explained that she needed to pack up the house first and that she was hoping it would sell quickly, given its location to the university.

"So realistically, a couple of months, I think. There's something else though," Lianne said, holding out her left hand. "I got engaged at Christmas!"

"Oh, my goodness that is fantastic news Lianne, I am so happy for you!" Helen got up from her seat and enveloped Lianne in a massive hug. "Wow, look at that ring! It's absolutely gorgeous and you so deserve this. I know you've had a rough couple of years and it's time things improved for you. And here you are about to marry a dishy Italian doctor! You look so happy Lianne, congratulations to you both!"

"Thank you, thank you. I am happy, I really am. But I must say that you and the company have been so good about everything, giving me time off when I needed to be with Mam, and allowing me to work from home. Most companies would have kicked me out, so I really am grateful."

"Lianne, you're an important part of this company and it would have been very short sighted of us not to give you all the help and support you needed."

Lianne thanked Helen again and they then turned the conversation to the business. By the time Lianne left Helen's office, half an hour later, she was absolutely starving and decided to pop out and grab something to eat. There was a long queue at the nearest sandwich shop, so she decided to venture a little further.

She was busy texting Gemma to see if she fancied meeting up later, when she walked straight into a guy walking towards her, who was also staring at his phone screen.

"I'm so sorry I…" Lianne said and as she looked up, she saw that the person she'd bumped into was Grant. "Oh, Hi. How are you?"

"I'm really well thanks, just come from the Court, needed to grab something to eat before the Court resumes." Grant was rather aloof, as he always was, trying to make out that he was a lot more important than he actually was.

"I won't keep you then," Lianne replied and went to move off.

"No, don't go." The tone of Grant's voice changed "It's nice to see you again, how are you? How's your Mam?"

"Mam's dead."

"Oh my God, I'm so sorry Lianne I didn't know, honestly. I would have been in touch if I'd known."

"That's OK, no reason why you should know."

"Look I was just going to grab a sandwich, why don't we go and get a coffee and something to eat, and you can tell me what happened."

Lianne was reluctant to agree, but Grant was quite persistent and he did genuinely seem to care about what had happened. "OK, but I don't have that long, as I need to be back at work by 2:00 p.m."

They made their way to a nearby coffee shop and were fortunate enough to arrive, just as a young family was leaving so they grabbed the table.

"You sit there Lianne, and I'll get the coffees. I'll also ask someone to come and clean the table."

Lianne sat down and shortly after, a young lady appeared, to remove the dirty cups and clean the table. "Thank you," Lianne said and the woman looked at her, as if no one had ever thanked her before.

After about 5 minutes, Grant returned with the coffees and 3 packs of sandwiches.

"I got tuna mayo, ham salad, or cheese and tomato. I wasn't sure what you'd like, so just help yourself." Lianne thanked him and picked up the tuna sandwich. "I'm really sorry about your Mam Lianne, I honestly didn't know she'd passed. You were so close; you must be devastated. You know I used to be jealous of your relationship with your Mam, I have two parents at home and neither have any interest in me or my life, not like your Mam. What happened?"

Lianne explained all about the Motor Neurone Disease, how it had affected her Mam and the impact it had had.

"She died about 10 months ago now. It's strange, sometimes it seems like yesterday and other times it feels as if it was years ago."

"I'm so sorry," Grant said, sounding as if he genuinely did care, "and it's not as if you know your dad, so it must be really hard."

"Actually, when Mam passed, I found some old letters and actually tracked down my dad, he didn't even know I existed, as Mam had never told him. And I have three half siblings!"

"Bloody hell, that's amazing! Does he live around here?"

"No, he's Italian, Mam met him when she was on holiday there."

"I don't suppose you'll get to see much of him then, with him being so far away."

"Well actually, I'm moving to Italy soon, as I'm getting married!"

Grant looked genuinely shocked, and it seemed like an eternity before he spoke "Well…congratulations, I'm really pleased for you, I hope you'll be very happy."

The whole tone of Grant's voice and his demeanour changed, to an outsider it would have been perfectly clear that he was still carrying a torch for Lianne and had hoped to get back into her good books by supporting her. Finding out not only that Lianne was moving away but that she was marrying some pasta eating doctor, was like a knife through the heart.

"Well, I really am very pleased for you. Oh shit, look at the time! I really must get back to the Court, can't keep the judge waiting! Nice to see you, Lianne." And with that, he was out of his seat and out the door before Lianne could say anything. She smiled to herself, there was a time when she would have cared about Grant and his feelings, but not anymore. He was her past and Ricardo was her future.

She finished her coffee and as she did, her phone pinged.

Definitely on for a catch up usual place at 6?xx

Lianne quickly replied and then headed back to work.

"Jeezzz! Grant! He's the last person you needed to see!" Gemma said when Lianne told her what had happened at lunchtime. "He must be gutted that you're not pining after him, and worse than that you have the audacity to marry some good looking, hunky, Italian doctor!" Gemma laughed.

"I hardly think he's still interested in me! I'm sure he's moved on to some other poor unsuspecting woman."

"Anyway, enough about him. Tell me all about the proposal and the wedding and everything else!"

Lianne told Gemma everything that had happened in Italy, how she'd met her dad, her two half-sisters and her half-brother.

"That must have been really weird."

"It was! I was so nervous beforehand, and I think Mia, the eldest, was a bit suspicious about it all. But to be honest, I look so much like Gabriella, it's quite frightening. I think there's still a long way to go before they really accept me, but that's OK. Maybe the wedding will help to bring us all together."

"Oh yes, the wedding!" Gemma said, with a high-pitched shriek that caused several people in the pub to turn around. "I want to know everything!"

"It's going to be very quiet and small," Lianne replied. "I'd like to get married in a church in Italy if that's possible, and I'll expect you to be my maid of honour!" Gemma shrieked again as Lianne continued. "We're also going to look to buy somewhere bigger, Ricardo's apartment is lovely but it's not a family home. And before you say anything, no I'm not pregnant! But we want to have kids so we'll need a bigger place."

"Will you sell the house here?" Lianne nodded "I suppose it makes sense, there's no point hanging on to the house if you're going to be living over there. Oh Lianne, I'm so pleased for you." And with that Gemma hugged Lianne tightly.

The girls carried on chatting for another hour or so before heading home. Once again, they hugged each other and agreed that they would meet up again in a few weeks.

Chapter 30

The estate agent called over on the Saturday morning and took some pictures and measurements of the house. He seemed to make lots of noises as he went around, "Mmm yes", "Oh dear", "Ah yes". Lianne had no idea what it all meant, she knew the house needed work but was realistic about what the property was worth.

"Well, Miss Reynolds, the house obviously needs a bit of work, but it would be an excellent investment for anyone looking to rent the house out to students. I think we could get £400,000 for it without too much difficulty. So I would suggest we market it at £425,000, and see what happens. We can always lower the price if we need to."

Lianne was genuinely surprised by the figures being quoted—house prices had obviously gone up since she last checked.

"That sounds good to me, Mr Jackson. How quickly can you get it on the market?"

"It all happens very quickly these days, as it's all web based. If you're happy to sign the contract now, I can get the house online by tomorrow."

"That would be fantastic," Lianne replied. "I'm very happy to sign the paperwork now, if you have it with you."

The estate agent confirmed that he did and after a brief conversation about fees and advertising, Lianne signed the contract and he left.

When Lianne spoke to Ricardo later that day, she told him everything that the estate agent said.

"So, after fees and other costs, I should have about £350,000 to put down on a house in Lucca for us."

"This is very good news," Ricardo said, "but this not right. After I pay mortgage on apartment, I have about 200,000€ to buy house, so I think you not put in more than me and keep money for…how you saying, for day when it is raining."

Lianne laughed, "I'm very happy to put all my money into our new home, but I tell you what, why don't we wait and see what we can find, and then we'll sort out how much we need to put down."

Ricardo reluctantly agreed, and the conversation moved on to Ricardo's birthday which was at the end of January. Lianne would be in Lucca for his birthday weekend and she was really looking forward to it. She asked him if there was anything he'd like to do for his birthday, but he assured her that he just wanted to be with her.

"This is correct answer!" She said with a smile.

Lianne spent the rest of the weekend trying to sort through stuff. She would have to get rid of a lot of it when she moved. So, she might as well sort out what she wanted to keep and what she didn't. By Sunday evening, she had filled several black bags with rubbish that could go to the tip and numerous green bags with stuff for recycling. The process wasn't going quite as quickly as she'd hoped, as she kept getting distracted by things she found.

First there was a cardboard box with baby stuff in it and a second with cards and presents she'd made for her Mam over the years. She found projects she'd done in primary school on dinosaurs and 'my family'. The latter contained drawings she'd done of her Mam and what appeared to be some kind of super hero; she'd obviously been going through a stage of thinking her dad was Superman or something! Each discovery brought back happy memories and the odd tear. She knew she needed to be ruthless when sorting through things, but that was easier said than done.

When it came to sorting through ornaments, etc it was a little easier; very few pieces had any significance for Lianne, and she quickly amassed 2 large boxes of ornaments, and other bric a brac. She would keep a couple of pieces she particularly liked, but the rest could go to a charity shop. When it came to bedding and towels, again she only kept a few items; the bed linen could go to the Salvation Army, as they were always looking for bits and pieces to help people get back on their feet. Lianne was going to offer them most of the furniture too; there was one particular glass cabinet she would like to keep, but the rest of it really wasn't worth shipping to Italy.

By the time Sunday evening arrived, Lianne was exhausted but felt that she had made good headway clearing out things. When she spoke to Ricardo that evening, she told him what she had been up to, she told him of some of the things she'd found like her first pair of shoes and the Mother's Day cards that her Mam had kept.

"I've found so many things that I'd forgotten all about," she said, "it's really weird going through it all."

"This must be very hard also," he replied, "especially on your own."

"It is, but it's also strangely comforting, because it keeps Mam's memories alive. I know that sounds stupid, but it's like…I don't know…having proof that she was here."

"It not stupid, it important we have our memories. Will you bring these things to our new home?"

"Yes, if that's OK. I'll get rid of a lot of stuff, but there are somethings I want to keep."

"You no need to ask me! It will be your home and it important that you have your things here."

Lianne explained that she intended to have maybe one or two boxes of stuff that she'd have shipped over. Then it would just be her personal stuff and clothes to take over. They agreed that they would start looking at property the following weekend, when she was over. Ricardo had already spoken to a number of real estate agents in Lucca, and he hoped to have a number of properties for them to look at.

The next few days passed quickly. Lianne's house had gone up on the estate agent's website and he was reporting that there was already a lot of interest. Although Lianne took it all with a pinch of salt, she knew that estate agents were prone to exaggerating. However, as she waited in the airport for her flight on the Thursday, the estate agent called to arrange a number of viewings the following week.

As always, Ricardo was waiting as Lianne emerged into the arrivals hall and, as always, her heart started pounding as soon as she saw him. He swept her up and gave her a massive kiss before taking her through to the car park.

As they headed toward Lucca, Lianne explained that she made a good start on clearing out some of the stuff from the house. There wasn't that much of her Mam's stuff to go through, as Margaret had got rid of a lot of stuff before she became too ill. However, Lianne had found some stuff belonging to her grandparents. Her Mam never really talked about them other than to say that they had been very strict and had died before she was born. Lianne also told Ricardo that the estate agent had lined up 3 viewings for the following week, so the house could sell quickly.

"I have make arrangements for us to see four houses on Saturday and then we see my Mama on Sunday if this is OK for my birthday."

"That's great," Lianne replied, "what are the houses like?" Ricardo produced several sheets of paper with the details of each of the properties, which Lianne scanned. She couldn't read any of the blurb, but thought they looked really nice.

"Especially the newer one with the massive kitchen," she said. "I can't wait to see them, but for now I just want to get home and climb into bed with you for a massive cwtch."

"What is this word?" Ricardo asked. "I am not knowing it."

"Cwtch is definitely a Welsh word," she said with a laugh, "it means to cuddle up with some one!"

"Then am wanting this cwtch also!" He exclaimed.

Ricardo headed off to work on the Friday, and Lianne did some shopping, then in the evening they went out for something to eat and discussed the properties they were going to view the next day. They weighed up the pros and cons of each on paper and agreed that the highest they were prepared to pay for any house was 600,000€. One of the houses was considerably less than that, but it was clear that it needed a lot of work.

The first house they viewed on the Saturday was a definite no, the rooms were much smaller than the estate agent's blurb suggested and there was very little outside space. The second was the older house that needed renovating; the owner had passed away and it was clear that nothing had been done on the house for many years. But the rooms were a good size and the house certainly had a lot of potential. It still retained much of the original character and there was a lot of space at the back of the house and to the side. It was in a slightly elevated position, and so the views of Lucca and the surrounding area were lovely. Lianne and Ricardo both agreed that it had a lot going for it.

House number three, was also an older house but it had already been renovated. However, they were disappointed to find that all the original character had been ripped out leaving it feeling almost soulless. Then it was the turn of number 4; a relatively new property situated a little further out of Lucca. It had all been very tastefully done with 4 good size bedrooms, 2 living areas and a large kitchen diner. The garden was a reasonable size with a small pool and patio area. Lianne fell in love with the kitchen, which she knew she would. There was just so much space and there was a light and airy feel to it. She could almost see herself standing in the kitchen cooking a meal, as Ricardo came home from work, with 2 or 3 little ones running around. She was still in her daydream, when she realised Ricardo was talking to her.

"Sorry… I was miles away!"

"Si! I say this is very nice house but wonder if it too far from my office."

"Maybe."

The estate agent who was accompanying them then launched into his spiel about the advantages of living further out of Lucca, according to Ricardo, when he spoke to Lianne later in the car. They had another look around and left to check out the area in the car. It was certainly beautiful, but there were few amenities so two cars would be essential.

Later that evening, after they'd eaten, they had another long chat about the houses. There were really only 2 in the running, the newer house or the one in need of renovation. Lianne was clearly drawn to the former, but Ricardo thought it was worth considering the older house.

"If we buy the old house, we have chance to make it special, to make it what we want. I think it worth looking at what we could do and how much it would cost."

"I'm very happy to do that if you want, I just think it would be easier to move into a house that's already done."

"Si, but also I worry about time it take to get to my patients especially when everyone driving to work."

"OK," Lianne said, "do you know anyone who could look at it for us and give us a price? Maybe we could ask Alfonso if he could look at it too, he may have some ideas."

"This is very good idea. Shall you telephone him now?" Lianne agreed and after the usual chit chat in English, Ricardo spoke to Alfonso about the house they'd seen and the possibility of completely restoring it.

They spoke for nearly 10 minutes and Ricardo said he would email him a link to the details of the property, so that he could take a look and maybe come up with a few ideas. After they'd finished talking about the house, Lianne spoke to her dad again and agreed that they would meet up in 2 weeks, when Lianne came back over.

The Sunday was Ricardo's birthday, and they spent the day with Sofia, who, as always, cooked them a fabulous lunch. They showed her the information they had on the houses and explained that they had whittled it down to the 2; either the modern house which was ready to move into, or the older property which they could renovate to create something personal. Sofia agreed that she could see the merits of both and they agreed that a lot would depend on what they could realistically do with the house, and how much it would all cost.

Chapter 31

The next couple of weeks passed quickly. There were 3 viewings of Lianne's house and someone made an offer of £350,000 which the estate agent strongly suggested she reject. He said he knew the potential buyer and he made a habit of making ridiculous offers before eventually offering a reasonable amount. Lianne thought about the offer and agreed it was a little low and as the house had only been on the market for just over a week, it would be silly to take the first offer she'd received.

Lianne continued to pack up the house when she wasn't working and at the weekend, she took a load of stuff to the tip, she also arranged for someone from the Salvation Army to come and look at the furniture. Apart from the one glass cabinet that she wanted to keep, the rest needed to be found a new home and the Salvation Army said that they had lots of people who could make good use of what she didn't want.

Just before Lianne was due to fly back to Italy, there was another viewing on the house and she was offered £395,000, which she was happy to accept, so she had good news when Ricardo met her at the airport that evening.

"This excellent news," he said, "this mean you move to Italy very soon!"

"I suppose it does," Lianne said with a smile.

On the Friday evening, Lianne cooked and as they ate, Ricardo said that he'd been in touch with Alfonso and a friend of Marco's, who was a builder about the older house. They had come up with some ideas about what could be done with the house and the sort of cost they'd be looking at, if they decided to go for a full renovation.

Lianne was a little disappointed, although she said nothing to Ricardo; she really did have her heart set on the modern house and she had thought that he was making arrangements for them to have a second look over the weekend. They had even talked about it when they had Face-Timed earlier in the week, and they both seemed to be on the same wavelength, the more modern house would be a perfect home for them, and whilst it would mean a longer commute for Ricardo, they could literally move straight in. So, what Ricardo said next came as a complete shock.

"Alfonso has some incredible ideas about the house and he say we can restore fully and keep the…how you say…caratteristica."

"Character," she replied. "I thought we were going to see the new house again."

"Si, si. But tomorrow we see Alfonso and he show us what we can do. If you still want to see other house afterwards, then I take you."

Lianne was completely taken aback. One, she was going to see her dad again and two, it was clear that he and Ricardo had been working a lot on the idea whilst she was in Cardiff. Ricardo explained that he'd arranged to meet Alfonso at the property at 11:00 a.m. the next day and asked her to just keep an open mind, which she agreed to do, however she was concerned that she'd been kept completely out of the loop. Ricardo seemed to sense her unease.

"I know we not talk about old house but Alfonso ring me today so this new to me also."

Lianne nodded. "Okay."

They arrived at the house a little early, but Alfonso was already there and had picked up the key from the estate agent. He greeted Lianne with an enormous hug and shook Ricardo's hand.

"This very exciting," he said, "the house very strong and would make excellent home."

They headed inside and once again Lianne was struck by the space both inside and out, with so many original features, it was so much more than a series of boxes. Alfonso put some papers down on an old dining table and arranged them to show what he thought could be done. He wanted to retain the original staircase in the hall and then reconfigure the downstairs to create a large lounge with patio doors leading on to the garden, the lounge would retain the original stone fireplace and the cornice.

There would be a second living room which, Ricardo hinted could be a play room, a downstairs bathroom with a large walk-in shower, and then an extension on the side would create a large, open plan kitchen and dining area. Upstairs, there would be 3 large bedrooms and one smaller one, there would be a family bathroom as well as an en-suite off the master.

Lianne and Ricardo were amazed by what Alfonso had come up with. By retaining many of the original fixtures, such as the fireplaces and the old wooden doors, the house would be modern and practical, but maintain its character. Despite her earlier uncertainty about it all, Lianne was astounded, she had never expected or imagined that the house could look anything like this.

"Also," Alfonso said, "I have film you see." He opened up his iPad and played a short video which was literally a walk through the house when it was finished. It looked fantastic and the house was barely recognisable from the inside.

At that point, the estate agent returned for the key and it was agreed that Alfonso, Lianne and Ricardo would head to a nearby cafe to discuss things further.

Over a cup of coffee, Alfonso explained—mainly in Italian—that he had spoken to someone about planning permission and that shouldn't be a problem.

"I also speak with Roberto about money, he say all work on house cost about 150,000€ and 200,000€ to do garden area and make swimming pool. This include kitchen as I show you, bathrooms and full air conditioning system. What you think?"

Lianne and Ricardo both started to talk at once! "Mi scusi, you speak Lianne."

"I have to admit the drawings look amazing and the house would have everything we want with plenty of space to grow."

"Sono d'accordo," Ricardo said, "the house be beautiful home. How long would work take?"

Alfonso explained that Roberto had indicated that the work could be done in about 4–5 months if it was empty. Lianne and Ricardo agreed that they needed to give it a lot of thought, as it would be a huge commitment but they were very grateful for all the work Alfonso had done.

The conversation then moved on to Lianne's siblings and she said that she had been pleased with the way things had gone at Christmas and she asked Alfonso what they had said about her.

"Mia still find it strange she no eldest now; Lorenzo he no say much he—" Alfonso made a typical teenage boy's grunting sound and Lianne laughed. "Gabriella she think you wonderful and she tell all her friends about her new sister."

"I'm glad they're OK," Lianne said, "it must be very hard for them, having a complete stranger turn up on their doorstep. I really hope we can meet again soon."

"I think this excellent idea, maybe when you come to Lucca next."

The conversation then moved on to the wedding; no date had been set, but both Lianne and Ricardo liked the idea of having a small family wedding with a party at their new home afterwards, which Alfonso thought was a lovely idea.

When it was time to leave, Alfonso hugged Lianne again and as she did, so she said "Can I call you Babbo?" Alfonso nodded and a tear ran down his cheek and he held Lianne even tighter.

That evening, Lianne and Ricardo went out to eat and had a long conversation about the house. Having seen what could be achieved they were both were really keen, but it would mean keeping the apartment on while the work was being done on the house, and so Ricardo wouldn't be able to put any money into the work. The house was on the market for 380,000€ and had been up for sale for a while, so they felt certain that they could get it for nearer 350,000€.

If they got a 50% mortgage, Lianne said she could pay the remainder and would still have the cash to pay for the work. Ricardo wasn't very happy at the prospect of Lianne footing the bill, but they agreed it was the only way it could be done, and as Lianne said, once the apartment was sold, he could repay her if he insisted.

They agreed to think about it for the rest of the weekend and make a decision by the Monday, when Lianne would be heading back to Cardiff.

When they met with Sofia the next day, they told her all about the house and showed her Alfonso's drawings. Lianne also told her about the newer house they'd seen which they could move into without the need to do any work, and asked for her opinion.

"Modern house very nice, very…how you say…clinico. Old house need much work but everything be your choice."

"I guess so, I think I'm just worried about the work that's needed."

But Sofia's words got Lianne thinking, buying the older house would certainly give them the opportunity to create what they wanted. If they opted for the newer house, they wouldn't have any money to do anything to it, not that it really needed work, but they wouldn't be able to personalise it.

By the time Ricardo was driving Lianne back to the airport the following day, they had agreed that they'd put an offer in on the old house and see what happened. As Lianne sat quietly on the flight back, she started to feel really excited at the prospect of essentially designing her own home.

When Lianne was able to turn her phone back on, there was a message from Ricardo to let her know that he'd put in an offer of 340,000€, so all they could do now was wait. And, just as she was parking her car outside the house, she had another message to say they'd agreed a figure of 345,000€.

"OMG!" She said out loud, "we've just bought a house!" And with that, she headed in, with a beaming smile on her face.

Chapter 32

When Lianne returned to Italy about 10 days later, she had packed up everything she wanted to keep and had arranged for the stuff to go into storage until they were able to move into their new home. The sale of the house was going through without any problems and Lianne had arranged for the Salvation Army to come and clear the house. They helped so many families, and whilst the furniture wasn't modern, it was in good condition and practical, so she was certain they'd find good homes for it all.

She had sorted everything out with work and so the intention was, that she would take a few days annual leave but then start working from the apartment. It was all quite exciting and she was looking forward to sourcing Italian suppliers, although she really did need to learn Italian first! Saying goodbye to Gemma had been hard, although Lianne tried to reassure herself that they'd still meet up whenever she flew back to Cardiff for work, and they could always FaceTime with a bottle of wine each, if they needed a proper chat.

Lianne also felt a little happier knowing that Gemma had started seeing someone; it was someone she had literally bumped into in the coffee shop and she'd ended up spilling her coffee. He offered to buy her another and that as they say was that. Lianne felt certain that Brad would be taking up a lot of Gemma's time for the foreseeable future, so she felt a little less guilty.

Diane was sad to see her go, but again Lianne assured her that she would see her whenever she was back in Cardiff, and she expected Diane to visit her in Italy.

Getting off the plane in Italy was certainly a significant moment, it was strange, but as Lianne said to Ricardo later, it felt completely different even though she'd taken that same flight, etc so many times before. Maybe it was because she had more luggage this time, as she'd brought all her summer clothes as well as a few warmer things for the next month or so. Ricardo had cleared out one of the wardrobes for her, as well as a set of chest of drawers, so it all felt quite strange when she unpacked.

She usually kept a few bits and pieces in a drawer in the bedroom, so that she only needed hand luggage when she flew back and fore, but this time it was a whole wardrobe of clothes, as well as jewellery and some photos in frames that she put on the bedside table.

"Benvenuto a casa amore mio. Welcome home my love," Ricardo said, as he poured them each a glass of wine a little while later "Benvenuto a casa."

That weekend it had been arranged, that Alfonso, Mia, Lorenzo and Gabriella were going to visit Lianne and Ricardo in Lucca. The apartment really wasn't big enough to accommodate everyone, certainly not for a meal, so Ricardo had booked a table in a restaurant, about 10 minutes' walk away.

Lianne was so excited when they arrived at the apartment, she hadn't seen her siblings since Christmas and she was keen to bond with them a little more. Thankfully it was a lovely spring day and whilst it was a little chilly, the sky was blue with a few fluffy clouds, so the doors on to the veranda were open creating more space.

Lorenzo didn't have much to say for himself, and Lianne got the feeling that he was there under sufferance! However, Mia and Gabriella certainly seemed pleased to see Lianne again; they chatted as best they could about the house and of course, the wedding. In the meantime, Ricardo and Alfonso were talking about the house. The purchase was going through and Alfonso was putting together the planning application for the extension, he intended to leave the plans with them for the weekend, so they could make any changes they wanted before he prepared the final version.

After an hour or so, they all left to go to the restaurant and enjoyed the short walk in the sunshine. Their table was ready when they arrived and they each perused the menu. Ricardo ordered some wine and some water for the table, which was brought with a platter of antipasto which they all tucked into.

"You say your padre no longer with us?" Alfonso asked Ricardo.

"Si, Babbo is gone few years now, but Mama still here and live not far away. Also, my sister and her family."

"I think would be good to meet your Mama, she will be family when you are married."

"She would very much like that," Ricardo replied. "She love Lianne very much and want to meet her padre."

"Then we will make it happen. And we have wedding to plan!"

"Si, si. I have something to say, which is surprise for Lianne. She tell me you meet her Mama outside Chiesa di San Michele first time." Alfonso nodded. "I have speak with the Church and they say we can marry there. Would this make you happy Lianne?"

Lianne didn't need to answer, the tears were rolling down her cheeks "Oh my goodness…that would be amazing, it would be as if Mam was there with me," she sobbed. "Would you be happy about this Babbo?"

Alfonso didn't need to answer either, as there were also tears running down his cheeks. "I am thinking this will be excellent!"

"So," Ricardo said, "all we need to do now is set a date!"

It was a lovely weekend and it felt very strange when Lianne wasn't heading back to the airport on the Monday. She had decided that she'd like take a closer look at the plans and also do some research to get ideas for the kitchen and the bathrooms. She spent much of the morning on the internet and by lunchtime, she had a few ideas that she wanted to discuss with Ricardo.

After lunch, she Face-Timed Diane her and told her all about the weekend; she also told her about their intention to marry in the church where her Mam and dad had first met. Diane was literally in tears as Lianne told her what Ricardo had done.

"Ricardo is obviously a very nice man and thinks the world of you, to go to such lengths. Have you decided on a date yet?"

"Realistically," Lianne replied, "I think we're looking at next spring, as we'll want to settle into the new house before we get married. You will come to the wedding, won't you?"

"Of course, I'll be there, I need to check out this young doctor of yours!"

"Thank you. I really want you to meet my dad, and Ricardo of course!"

"Then I will be there, lovely girl," Diane replied. "How are you feeling about this week?" Diane continued.

"I have to admit I can believe it's been a year; it seems like only yesterday," she said, "but then on the other hand it feels as if Mam's been gone forever. So much has happened in the last year."

"It's not easy," Diane said, "but I think you'll find it's all a bit of an anti-climax and the anticipation is worse than the actual day. It's almost as if you expect the world to stop or something to happen to acknowledge the milestone, but of course it doesn't, everything just carries on as normal."

"I suppose it's just something I have to go through. This time, last year, my whole world fell apart, but now look at me—living in Italy, engaged to be married, and I've found my dad. I miss Mam terribly every single day, but I have a lot to be thankful for."

"You do lovely girl, you do."

That evening, Lianne told Ricardo what she'd found on the internet and they chatted about the ideas she had. She then told him that she'd Face-Timed Diane who thought he was a very kind, thoughtful person.

"She very clever lady!" Ricardo said with a laugh. "I am looking forward to meeting her. Did you have a good talk?"

"We did. We were talking about the fact that it's the first anniversary of Mam passing on Thursday and how my life has changed."

"I am not knowing about Thursday; I am glad you tell me. It will be hard but I will be here for you."

"Thank you. I don't really know how I feel about it all, I miss Mam so much but if I hadn't lost her, I wouldn't have found you."

"This is true but losing you Mama is very hard." With that, he put his arms around Lianne and she snuggled into his shoulder. "I am very sad for you that your Mama is gone but very happy for me that I have found you!"

As Diane had suggested the first anniversary was a bit of an anti-climax. Lianne had woken late as she hadn't slept well and Ricardo didn't want to disturb her. She lay in bed for a while and then opened the bedroom curtains. Just as Diane had said, life was carrying on regardless just as it had when she'd looked out of her Mam's bedroom window a year ago.

Lianne made some coffee and sat on the veranda to enjoy the early spring sunshine. She turned on her phone and there were a few messages from friends and Diane hoping she was alright. And she was alright; as she sat there, she knew she would be OK, she had Ricardo and now she had a dad and siblings.

She found a picture of her Mam on her phone; it was one of her favourites; they'd both been working in the small back garden and Mam had a big smudge of mud on her face, but she was happy and smiling, and that was the Mam Lianne wanted to remember now.

"I miss you Mam so much," she said out loud, "but I've found Alfonso and he still remembers you, he says you were his first love and he never forgot you. And I'll never forget you Mam, never." With that, the tears started to roll down her cheeks and she let them; she had every right to cry if she wanted to.

A little later, Lianne went for a walk, it was a beautiful day and she was out for a few hours enjoying the sunshine. She stopped for a coffee and a cake as she watched the world go by and then headed back to the apartment. She'd only been home about half an hour, when Ricardo came home considerably earlier than expected. He was carrying a huge bouquet of red roses and he said he just wanted her to know how much he loved her.

Lianne put the flowers in water, and they both sat on the veranda. There was no real need for conversation, it was nice to just sit there in silence holding hands. Eventually the silence was broken by Lianne's phone; it was Diane Face-Timing her. Ricardo left her to it and went into the apartment to make a start on dinner.

When they went to bed later that night, Ricardo again put his arms around her and held her close. "Thank you," she said, "for letting me be me today. I love you."

"I love you too," he replied and as he did so Lianne drifted off into a deep sleep.

Chapter 33

Lianne started back to work the following Monday and the first thing she did when she logged into the company system was to send her boss Helen a photo of the view from the veranda where she'd set up the computer. The photo was of a clear blue sky and the rooftops of Lucca, with the comment "my new office!" Helen quickly sent back a view from her office window of a cold, wet Cardiff and a brick wall, which made Lianne laugh.

Lianne spent the morning catching up on emails, she went for a short walk at lunchtime and then made some tentative enquiries about potential Italian suppliers in the afternoon. By the time Ricardo returned from work, she was buzzing, having made a couple of appointments for the following week.

They sat down to eat, about an hour later, and Ricardo explained that the planning application had gone in for the house, so all they could do now was wait. They weren't envisaging any problems as the proposals wouldn't affect any of the neighbouring properties, but it would still take a couple of months for the application to be processed, and until it was approved, there was nothing they could do.

"Do you think we should look to set a date for the wedding?" Lianne asked "Even a small wedding will take some planning, what do you think?"

"I very happy to make date, do you have idea?"

"I was thinking of April or early May next year, before it gets too hot. What do you think?"

"This very good time. We will need to speak to the Church to see what date is empty. I can phone Church tomorrow if you happy with this."

Lianne had a big beaming smile on her face, "I am happy; very, very, very happy!"

A few days later, the date had been confirmed—they would marry on 29th April the following year, at Chiesa di San Michele and would have a small reception afterwards at their new home. They had made contact with a number of caterers and eventually opted for someone Sofia knew of; it was all coming together very nicely.

A couple of weeks later Lianne, Ricardo and his family drove to Bologna to meet Alfonso and his family. It was a perfect day, weather wise, and they spent most of the day in the garden, with Isabella's children running around like idiots, playing with Alfonso's two dogs. Alfonso had decided to do a barbecue and Sofia had insisted on preparing a number of dishes to add to the feast they were enjoying.

As they finished eating, Lianne told everyone that they had fixed the date for the wedding and she outlined the plans for the reception. Everyone was excited, and immediately the women started talking about colour schemes!

Then Lianne turned to Alfonso, "Will you walk me down the aisle Babbo?" she asked.

"Si, si!" He answered. "I very honoured to stand beside you. I just hope the house ready!"

The wedding chat continued for most of the afternoon for the women, whilst the men focussed on the plans for the house. Alfonso explained in detail for Lorenzo and Emilio what they were hoping to do, both were very impressed and even Lorenzo commented on what his dad had designed, saying that it would be nice to see his dad's ideas come to life.

Later in the afternoon, Alfonso and Sofia were sat together outside watching the children playing. "It must be very strange for you to suddenly have a daughter in your life, that you knew nothing about," Sofia said.

"Very strange," came the reply. "I honestly never forgot Lianne's Mama, Maggie was my first love and I was devastated when she stopped answering my letters. Deep in my heart I knew there had to be a very good reason why she wasn't writing to me anymore, but I never thought she was pregnant, it never crossed my mind."

"How did your children react to the news, honestly?"

"Like me, they were shocked, especially with them having lost their own Mama the year before. They were all very suspicious, although I don't quite know why, it's not as if I've got a fortune stashed away. Mia was the most suspicious and she wanted me to insist on a DNA test, but as soon as I saw Lianne, I knew she was mine. It took me a long time to persuade her to meet Lianne, but once she had, her suspicions faded. As for Lorenzo, he is a typical teenage boy and doesn't care about anything, and Gabriella was just excited about it all, especially when Lianne looked so much like her."

"It must have been very difficult, but I have to say Lianne is a lovely girl, she's very thoughtful and considerate and I know she would have walked away, if you or the children hadn't wanted her in your lives. But I think she's a great addition to both our families and hopefully one day there will be some little bambinis!"

"Si, si!" and with that, they both laughed and hugged each other.

By early evening, it was time to leave. Isabella had put the children in their pyjamas knowing they would quickly fall asleep in the car, and she could then simply lift them into bed. Everyone thanked Alfonso for his hospitality and agreed that they must all do it again soon, but this time at Sofia's.

Lianne felt quite overcome by it all, this time last year, she knew none of these people yet here they were—her new family; it was quite surreal.

About 6 weeks later, the planning committee contacted Alfonso about the proposals for the house and insisted on a few minor changes, but nothing of any significance, and the day before Lianne's birthday, Alfonso telephoned to say that the plans had been approved. It was a huge relief to them all and Alfonso wanted to instruct the builder to start working on it as soon as possible; the sale of Lianne's house in Cardiff had been finalised a few weeks beforehand so the money was there to get things moving.

It was also incredibly exciting and Lianne spent a lot of her spare time looking at kitchens, bathroom suites, tiles, flooring, etc. It was all beginning to feel really real and each time they went to the house they could see the progress that was being made.

Both Diane and Gemma had been excited to know that a date had been set for the wedding, and something Gemma said prompted Lianne to make arrangements to fly back to Cardiff to go wedding dress shopping with them both. She had been so caught up with the house that she'd been oblivious to the fact that time was passing and she needed to find something to wear so that there would be enough time for the gown to be ordered and any alterations made.

Lianne flew back to Cardiff one Friday afternoon; because the house had been sold, she had nowhere to stay, so Gemma offered her, her spare room. It was a little small, but it was only for a couple of nights. They spent the evening catching up on all the latest gossip and it was just like old times. They shared a bottle of wine with a Chinese takeaway and put the world to rights. They crawled into bed just after midnight, and when the alarm went off at 7:30 a.m. Lianne felt like "death warmed up", as her Mam used to say.

The first of 3 appointments were booked for 9:30 a.m. and Diane was waiting outside the shop, when Lianne and Gemma arrived.

She enveloped Lianne in a massive hug, "It's so good to see you, it seems like ages since I last saw you!"

"I know, it's crazy," came the reply. "I live and work in Italy now!"

The three carried on chatting, as they knocked on the door and waited. A tall slim woman with flaming red hair answered the door and announced that she was Eleanor and would be Lianne's consultant for the appointment. As they entered the store, they were astounded at the sheer number of wedding dresses on display; it was a bit like the tardis—it looked small from the outside but was huge inside. Eleanor left them for a few minutes to let them browse through the racks, and when she returned, she asked Lianne if she had any idea of what she wanted, what style, colour, and most of all budget.

"I'd like to keep it under £2,000, if I can," Lianne answered, "but if it's absolutely perfect, I can go a little higher. I have idea about what style, but I don't want anything too flashy and I'd like to stick with an ivory or cream."

"Okay, that sounds great, why don't your entourage take a seat, you go to the changing room and get undressed and I'll pull a few dresses for you to start things off."

Lianne disappeared into the changing room and Eleanor reappeared about 5 minutes later.

"So, what I want to do," she said, "is try a number of different styles so we can see what you feel most comfortable in."

The first dress Lianne tried on was a typical princess ball gown; the bodice was embellished with crystals and had a sweetheart neckline. As she walked out to where Diane and Gemma were waiting, she couldn't believe the weight of it! There were lots of "oo's" and "ah's" as she walked out, and Diane even had a tear in her eye but Lianne knew it wasn't for her.

"I do like it," she said, "and I think it looks really pretty, but it's just not me! There's far too much of it and in the heat, I think it would be a nightmare."

Diane seemed a little disappointed, but Gemma agreed that it just wasn't Lianne. The next dress was what they called a fishtail and it was like being laced into a straight-jacket!

"Va va voom!" Gemma exclaimed as Lianne appeared, "If you're going for the sex goddess look, then I think it's perfect!"

"Wow," Diane said. "I didn't know you were hiding that figure under your jeans and sweatshirt! I have to say you look absolutely stunning, but I'm not sure it's you."

Lianne agreed, she wasn't the sort of person to flaunt herself in public, even when she was younger and used to go to nightclubs with Gemma.

The third dress was a lot more along the lines of what Lianne was thinking of, it was a very soft fabric with a little lace and crystals on the bodice that petered out the further down the dress you went; it was fitted at the top and then draped from the hips, and the back was open with what looked like a spiderweb of thin crystal straps. Lianne absolutely loved it. Both Diane and Gemma were blown away when Lianne walked out, and they could see by the look on her face that she felt the same.

"So," Eleanor said, "what do you think?"

"I love it," came the reply, "it's simple but elegant and perfect for an Italian wedding."

"You look amazing!" Gemma said, "the shape really suits you and there's just enough bling."

Diane couldn't really speak and in between tears all she could say was, "Beautiful, just beautiful!"

They chatted a little more, and Eleanor confirmed that the dress cost £1,700 so was within budget, but Lianne just didn't know what to do.

"Oh, I don't know! What do you think I should do? What about our other appointments? I just can't decide!"

"Look," Eleanor said helpfully, "it's important that you feel 100% happy before you make a decision. If you have other appointments, then go to them, this dress isn't going anywhere, so if you decide that it's 'the one', then just let me know and we'll order it."

"Is that OK?" Lianne asked. "I feel awful, as if I'm messing you around."

"Not at all, it's absolutely fine. Come on let's get you out of the dress."

A short while later, they all left the store and headed for their next appointment, thanking Eleanor for all her help. The second store was only a short distance in the car and Lianne knew from the moment that she walked in that she wasn't going to find anything. All the dresses were terribly expensive with even the plainest gown costing more that she wanted to spend. She tried on 3 or 4 dresses but none of them were worth blowing her budget for.

When they left the store, they went to a nearby pub where Lianne had booked a table for them to have some lunch. As they ate, she told Diane and Gemma all about the house and she showed them Alfonso's 'vision'. She also shared a load of photos of Alfonso and her siblings and Diane was struck by how similar Lianne and Gabriella were.

"Wow!" She said. "I always thought you must look like your dad and there's no doubt you're Gabriella's sister."

"I know, it's crazy. Mia looks more like her Mam, from the photos I've seen of her, and Lorenzo is very much like Alfonso when he was young. It's really weird going from being an only child to suddenly having a brother and sisters. There's been this whole other family that have been there the whole time but I knew nothing of them!"

They carried on chatting for a while and then headed out to their third and final appointment. The store was situated on the outskirts of Cardiff and Gemma said she knew several women at work who had bought their dresses there. As they entered, they were overwhelmed by the sheer number of dresses available and they all started to browse through the racks. The consultant greeted them and after chatting to Lianne about the style of dress that she wanted she sent Lianne through to the changing room.

All four dresses Lianne tried on were similar in style to the one she liked in the first store but none of them made her feel the way she had done in the original dress. One had far too much bling, another was too clingy and would show every 'lump and bump'; whatever Lianne tried on there was no 'wow' moment, no tears, and with each dress Lianne was even more certain that she'd found her dress earlier in the day, and her entourage agreed. So, as they left the store, they headed back to the first one to order the dress.

Eleanor didn't seem to be surprised when Lianne knocked the door and she greeted them all with a smile. Within about 10 minutes, the order was placed, the money paid, and Lianne was grinning from ear to ear.

She was still grinning when she Face-Timed Ricardo later.

Chapter 34

The work on the house was going well, and by mid-September things were starting to take shape. The kitchen had been ordered, as well as the bathroom suites, the flooring and the tiles. Lianne and Ricardo had been out looking at furniture and had decided on colour schemes for the lounge area and their bedroom; the others could wait until they were settled in.

A landscaper had drawn up plans for the outdoor area which would include a good-sized pool, and a large pagoda to shelter from the strong sunshine. There would be a small area for plants and bougainvillea growing alongside the one wall.

With the end in sight, it was time for Ricardo to put the apartment on market. He contacted a local estate agent and within days, there had been a few people to view it. It was always arranged around Lianne's work, so that there weren't strange people in the background if she was on a video call!

It came as no surprise when Ricardo had an offer on the apartment for the full asking price, less than a week after the property was listed. Whilst they were both delighted Lianne would be sorry to see it go, it was such a significant part of her life with Ricardo and she had so many memories of their time together in the apartment, but it needed to be sold and she and Ricardo would start a new life together in their own home.

By the beginning of November, they had started packing everything up in the apartment and they were moving things a bit at a time into the house. Most of the furniture was going with them and that would all be moved by professionals. Lianne had also arranged delivery of the items she had put into storage, when she'd sold her Mam's house. And by the end of the month, they had moved out of the apartment completely and into their house.

They were both amazed at what had been achieved with the house, you wouldn't recognise it as the same place they had seen earlier in the year. The rooms were light and spacious and Lianne said the kitchen looked like one of those you saw on the television with integrated appliances and more cupboard space than she ever thought she could fill!

Lianne particularly loved the hallway with the large open staircase, all the woodwork had been stripped back and varnished, giving it a really natural feel, and with the new doorway and glass panels there was so much light flooding in.

Their bedroom was enormous compared to what they had in the apartment and there was a good size en-suite bathroom. The decor was simple with pale grey and the occasional splash of turquoise. As they snuggled up in bed, that first night they were like a couple of naughty children, giggling and chatting until the early hours.

"I am so happy Ricardo, I really am. This house is incredible and I'm so glad you persuaded me to consider it."

"I think it is Babbo we thank, he have…how you say…la visione…to see what it could be."

"True. I was thinking that as a thank you, we could invite all your family and mine over on Boxing Day, and have a sort of house warming party. What do you think?"

"What is this house heating? I never hear of this before. Is it like the barbecue?"

"No, no no!" Lianne laughed. "It's just a celebration for when you move into a new home! A sort of party or fiesta in the house."

"Then I am liking this house warming!"

"And I am liking you!" Lianne said, kissing him gently at first and then more passionately.

Before they knew it, Christmas was upon them and this year, they decided to have a quiet day on their own, as they were seeing all the family the next day. Lianne spent most of the day baking and preparing for the party, so it wasn't very Christmassy, but in the evening, they sat down to a lovely meal and exchanged gifts. They had agreed beforehand that with the wedding to pay for and the new house, they would only buy small gifts for each other. Lianne bought Ricardo a beautiful leather briefcase, he was always carrying his notes and other stuff around in a tatty old case he'd had for many years. Then Ricardo produced a small box and gave it to Lianne.

"I hate to tell you this," Lianne said with a smile, "but I'm already engaged to someone else so there's no point in producing a ring!"

"Oh no! This is very bad news," Ricardo laughed. "But it is good, I am not asking you to marry me!"

Lianne opened the box and found a pair of sparkling diamond stud earrings, they were absolutely beautiful, not too big or flashy, just perfect. Then Lianne realised that these would have cost considerably more than they'd agreed.

"Ricardo, what have you done? They're absolutely gorgeous and I love them, but we agreed we'd only spend a little on presents this year."

"Si, si. They are very little!" He said smirking, and with that Lianne realised he'd deliberately misunderstood the use of the word 'little' or 'small'. She should be angry with him, but they were beautiful and she knew they were perfect and were the sort of thing she could wear every day.

"You are very naughty," she said, "but thank you."

"Si, si, I very naughty," he said laughing, and promptly picked her up and carried her to their bedroom…

Lianne was up early the next day to get a head start on preparing lunch; having such a large kitchen made things so much easier and she knew she would never have managed in the apartment. Lunch would be a buffet style and she'd prepared a variety of dishes, some of which just needed to be popped in the oven when everyone arrived. The remainder were either in the fridge or already set up on the table. Once she was satisfied that she'd done everything she could, she headed upstairs to have a shower and change.

When she came down 40 minutes later, she looked stunning in a baby blue jumpsuit, which she wore with navy flats. Her long dark hair was tied back in a loose plait and she was wearing the earrings Ricardo had given her the night before.

"Bellissima!" Ricardo said, as she walked into the kitchen. "I am very lucky man!"

"Yes, you are!" Lianne said, before kissing him gently on the lips.

With that, the doorbell rang, and it was Sofia, she had said she would come a little early in case Lianne needed a hand. She was blown away as she walked around the house. She'd seen photos of the original house and had viewed Alfonso's drawings and video numerous times, but the finished product was so much better than she had expected. The rooms all flowed and the colour schemes complemented each other. Every room you went into was simply furnished and filled with natural light. In the lounge, she spotted the glass cabinet that had belonged to Lianne's Mam and she could see why Lianne had wanted to keep it;

it was a semi-circular shape made of mahogany and glass with several glass shelves. There were just a few pieces of glass and china in the cabinet, and it was clear that each meant something to Lianne.

"The house is eccellente!" She said hugging Lianne. "It hard to believe it the same house!"

"I'm glad you like it, we're really pleased with it, aren't we Ricardo?"

Ricardo nodded and poured his Mama a drink. Sofia offered to help out with the food, but Lianne assured her that it was all under control. So, the three of them sat on the large settee situated at the end of the kitchen, which had come from the apartment. It wasn't long before the doorbell went again, and this time it was Alfonso with Mia, Lorenzo and Gabriella; a short time later Isabella and Emilio arrived with the three children.

After everyone had wandered around the house, Lianne announced that the food was ready and everyone tucked in. There was a good balance of Italian food as well as more British fare, and Lorenzo's eyes lit up when he spotted the Welsh cakes.

Once everyone had eaten, it was time for presents and soon the lounge was full of bits of wrapping paper, Isabella kept telling the children to pick it up and not throw it around, but Lianne assured her that it was absolutely fine. In fact, it reminded her of Christmases when she was a child. She would be so excited to think that Santa had been that she'd rip off all the wrapping paper desperate to see what Santa had got her. By the time she'd finished opening everything, you wouldn't be able to see the bed or the carpet for wrapping paper! Happy times.

The children played with their new toys and the adults sat around talking, Lianne's Italian was definitely improving and she was able to understand a lot of what people were saying now, although she was a little reluctant to speak Italian for fear of getting it wrong or mispronouncing words. But everyone was very complementary and thought she was doing well.

The conversation inevitably came round to the wedding, with only 4 months to go, it wouldn't be long. Apart from the family, there would only be a dozen or so guests. Diane and Gemma would be coming over from Cardiff and a couple of people from Lianne's work. Ricardo had invited a few close friends like Marco and his partners in the practice.

"You are very excited now?" Gabriella asked. "Do you have a dress?"

"Yes, I'm excited and yes I have a dress," Lianne answered. "I need to go back to Cardiff once more for my final fitting though, then I'll be done!"

"I am also very excited," Gabriella said. "Babbo has given money so Mia and I go shopping for dresses! I tell Babbo I need also shoes and bag, but he say no more money!"

Lianne laughed, "I'm sure you will find something!"

They started to talk then about the practicalities of the day. Alfonso and the children would drive to Lucca the day before and were staying at a hotel not far from the church. Ricardo would stay at Sofia's the night before, and Diane and Gemma were staying at the house with Lianne. Alfonso would then come to the house on the morning of the wedding to pick up Lianne.

After the service, everyone would return to the house and the caterers would sort out the food and drinks, with a small number of waiters or waitresses to pass round canapés, etc. The caterers would set out a number of small tables and chairs outside and so hopefully, if the weather was good, guests would spill out into the garden area.

The conversations continued into the early evening, at which point Alfonso said he needed to head back to Bologna. The others also felt it was time to make a move, they thanked Lianne and Ricardo for their hospitality and agreed that they should make it a family tradition to all meet up on Boxing Day.

By the time Lianne and Ricardo had finished clearing up and loading the dishwasher, it was nearly 9:00 p.m. and they decided to head up to bed.

"I think it went really well today, don't you?" Lianne asked, as she snuggled into him.

"It was excellente, just like you!" Came the reply.

"I'm so glad our families get on so well. It's crazy to think that this time last year, I hadn't met Mia, Lorenzo or Gabriella, and this time, 2 years ago, I didn't know any of you existed! It's really weird, now I have more family than I ever imagined." And with that thought, Lianne drifted off into a deep sleep.

Chapter 35

January was busy with work, as it always was. Lianne had sourced an Italian supplier who produced the most beautiful leather bags, all of which were slightly different, and the first order was being sent over to the Cardiff store, mid-January, ready for the new season. She'd also found a new supplier of knitwear, all of which had a very Mediterranean feel about them, and she was busy negotiating a deal to supply the store.

Mid-February Lianne flew back to Cardiff for her final dress fitting, once again, she stayed with Gemma who had now ended her relationship with Brad, after she found out he'd been cheating.

"So, I'm a free woman again," she informed Lianne. "Do you know if Marco is seeing anyone? He was rather cute wasn't he!"

"You're unbelievable! I expected to find you in floods of tears, mourning the end of your relationship and yet here you are lining up your next target!"

"Well, a girl can dream can't she!"

The dress fitting went well, there were a number of small alterations still to be made, and then the dress would be sent via a courier to Lianne in Italy. It was expected to arrive about 6 weeks before the wedding, so there wouldn't be any last-minute panic. It was all beginning to feel very real.

Ricardo's birthday was a quiet affair, they had seen Sofia the weekend beforehand, and so on the day, they just went out for a nice meal in a small trattoria not far from the house. They were both so busy with work and the wedding plans, that they didn't feel the need for a big celebration. Plus, Lianne was just recovering from an ear infection too and was still on antibiotics, so a quiet night suited them both.

After the meal, they walked back to the house and sat in the garden drinking coffee, wrapped up in blankets as it was chilly night. The sky was clear and Lianne was looking up at the stars, amazed at how many she could see.

"Wow! The sky is beautiful tonight, isn't it? There must be millions of stars up there!"

"Si, the sky very beautiful just like you," Ricardo replied taking hold of her hand. "I am very lucky man that soon I be your husband and you be my wife. I love you so much Lianne and cannot imagine my life without you."

"I love you too, very much," she said and with that she stood up and led him to the bedroom…

The wedding dress arrived at the end of March, and Lianne was relieved to see it. She'd had a couple of nightmares about it not arriving, or it was the wrong one and she'd had to get married in her pyjamas! So, she was really excited when it arrived and hung it up in one of the spare bedrooms, making Ricardo promise that he wouldn't go in there.

Everything was coming together nicely in respect of the wedding and so Lianne was able to focus on her work. There were a couple of projects she needed to finalise before the wedding, so it was full steam ahead. She had arranged to take the week off before the wedding, as Diane and Gemma would be arriving a few days early, so that Lianne could show them around. She knew Diane was keen to see the places her Mam had been, and where she'd met Alfonso. So, she had to get things sorted work wise in the next two weeks.

Lianne had identified a manufacturer of high-end menswear in Pisa, and she wanted to visit before the wedding to check the quality of the items and make sure that everything would be delivered on time, to the Cardiff store. Pisa wasn't far from Lucca, she'd driven to and from the airport there, numerous times. But it was a long day and there had been a few issues to sort out with the manufacturer, so by the time she got home that evening, she was exhausted. Ricardo had prepared them something to eat, but Lianne was just pushing it around her plate.

"You no like?" Ricardo asked.

"It's lovely, it really is, I'm just not very hungry I'm afraid. It's been a long day and I think I'm just over tired."

"You do too much, with wedding and work. I make you coffee and there still cake there you make."

"That sounds good, thank you, but I think I'll have tea rather than coffee."

"Si, I make tea. You sit down in lounge."

By the time Ricardo returned with the tea and cake, Lianne was fast asleep, so he lifted her up and carried her up to bed.

The following morning, Lianne was full of apologies. "I'm so sorry, falling asleep like that, I was just so tired."

"This is fine, you need sleep and I watch football!" Ricardo said with a smile.

"Well, I'm glad I didn't spoil your evening! I'm working from home today, so it'll be a quiet day."

"Bueno, I will see you later."

Lianne spent all day at her laptop sorting out numerous problems that seemed to have arisen, and before she knew it, it was gone 5:00 p.m. She realised she hadn't eaten all day, which explained why she was hungry so she made pasta in a creamy sauce with salmon and asparagus. The food was ready when Ricardo arrived home, and he was pleased to see her devour her meal, she also demolished a couple of Welsh cakes washed down with a cup of tea.

After they'd eaten, they chatted about her plans to show Diane around when she arrived. Diane and Gemma were flying over on the Tuesday and she would pick them up from the airport in Pisa. Lianne planned a quiet afternoon after their journey, and then in the evening, Diane would finally meet Ricardo. He admitted to being a little nervous, Diane was very important to Lianne and he wanted to make a good impression.

"Don't be so daft!" Lianne said, when Ricardo told her how he felt. "She's going to absolutely love you! And you've spoken to her on Face-Time so you're not complete strangers!"

"But meeting in person very different! I no want to let you down."

"You could never do that."

Chapter 36

Lianne found it quite strange to be the one waiting in the arrivals hall at Pisa airport. It made her realise how Ricardo must have felt waiting for the doors to open and hoping it was the person you were waiting for. Lianne had got to the airport early—even before the plane had landed—but she just didn't want to be late. She knew she'd have to wait awhile because Diane and Gemma were both bringing more than hand luggage, so they'd have to wait in the baggage hall.

Lianne's stomach was rumbling, she'd been so excited she couldn't face to eat anything before she left. So she headed to one of the numerous little cafes and ordered a pastry, she thought about getting a coffee too but decided to have a bottle of water instead.

Finally, she saw Diane and Gemma, as the sliding doors opened, her face lit up and she started crying, she was so happy.

"Hey! What's the matter?" Diane asked as she enveloped her in a massive hug.

"Nothing," Lianne spluttered. "I'm just so pleased to see you!"

"Come here," Gemma said, "what a big softy you are! Now don't make me cry or my mascara will run!"

Lianne laughed, and arm in arm the three of them headed to the car. Gemma had brought enough luggage for 2 weeks, but thankfully they managed to get all the bags in the car. As they headed out of the airport, the roads opened up and Diane could see the landscape, the sky was blue with just a few wispy clouds and everything looked stunning in the sunshine.

"Wow! Everything is so pretty," Diane said "I can see why you love it here."

"The scenery is stunning, but it's not just that, the people are so friendly and the pace of life is a lot slower. The family is a big thing over here, everything revolves around the family."

With that, Gemma did her Godfather impression and they all started laughing.

They carried on chatting about anything and everything and finally Lianne pulled into the driveway. They emptied the luggage out of the car and Lianne opened the front door. There were lots of appreciative noises, as Lianne showed them around the house and they took them to their rooms. Diane and Gemma both agreed that it was a beautiful house and a far cry from the terraced house Lianne had been brought up in, in Cardiff.

"I'm sure you're tired and hungry after your flight," Lianne said, "so why don't you unpack your bags, change if you want to, and then meet me in the kitchen when you're ready and we can have some lunch."

Half an hour later, the three of them were standing in the kitchen. Lianne had prepared a salad with cold meats and cheese and there was fruit and a tiramisu for dessert. It was a lovely day and not too hot, so they decided to eat in the garden. Lianne told them that she planned to take them into Lucca the next day, to show Diane around and before she could say anything, Gemma announced that she'd brought a pair of Converse sneakers with her, so there would be no repeat performance! Lianne laughed and reminded Diane that it had been Gemma's choice of footwear that had led her to meet Ricardo and ultimately to her finding her father.

The conversation then turned to the wedding and Lianne explained the plans for the day. "So, what about your hen do?" Gemma asked.

"I'm not bothering with anything like that," came the reply. "I'm pretty tired and really don't feel like a boozy hen do."

"Sorry, that's not the correct answer! But it doesn't have to be a boozy night, maybe we could just go for a meal, we ought to do something to celebrate your last days of freedom."

"Maybe," Diane said, "we could invite Ricardo's Mam and sister, it would be nice to meet them before the wedding."

"That's a great idea," Gemma said.

"That is a good idea, maybe Thursday evening. I think Ricardo is planning on having a few drinks with friends that evening anyway."

"That's settled then," Gemma said, "all you need to do now is speak to Ricardo's family."

The chat continued in the garden for several hours with Lianne catching up on all the news, and Gemma making them laugh with stories of her attempts to find Mr Right.

It was lovely for Lianne to spend time with them, they were the only 'family' that knew her before her Mam had died, before she met Ricardo. So many times, she'd think of something that had happened in her past or somewhere she'd been. She couldn't say things about her past to her new 'family', her memories and stories meant nothing to them. Sometimes it really hit home that in many respects she was an orphan; she may have now found her father now but he hadn't been a part of her life growing up. Her memories of Alfonso were all things that had happened in the last 18 months, nothing before that.

"Lianne, are you listening to me?" Gemma asked. "Hey, you're crying, are you OK?"

"Yes, I'm fine, just a bit overwhelmed, I think. Sorry I wasn't listening, what did you say?" "I was telling Diane about the time we…"

With that, Lianne starting laughing and they carried on reminiscing about their school days, much to Diane's amusement.

A short time later, Lianne heard the front door open and Ricardo come in, she called to let him know they were in the garden and he appeared a few moments later. He went straight over to kiss Lianne's forehead and then went to shake hands with Diane.

"Come here!" She said, giving him a massive hug. "I'm so pleased to finally meet you!"

"I am also very pleased to meet you, I know you very important to Lianne and that you always supporting her. So, I want you to know I take good care of her."

"I know you will and I think Lianne was very lucky to meet you."

Ricardo then turned his attention to Gemma, greeting her with kisses on both cheeks. "Ciao Gemma! It very good to see you again."

"And it's great to see you too!"

"Right," Lianne said. "I'm going to make a start on dinner and leave you three to talk!"

With that, Lianne headed back into the house and into the kitchen. She'd prepared a lasagne earlier, so just needed to put it in the oven and prepare the salad. She laid the table and then popped her head outside to let them know dinner would be about 45 minutes, and that she was heading upstairs for a shower.

Chapter 37

The following morning, Ricardo was up early and off to work, Lianne had got up with him and prepared breakfast for Diane and Gemma.

As they tucked in, Gemma noticed that Lianne wasn't eating much, she just seemed to be pushing the food around her plate.

"Are you OK, Lianne?" Diane asked. "You haven't eaten very much."

"Yes, I'm fine, just feeling a bit nauseous. It's just nerves."

Gemma laughed. "You're not pregnant, are you?"

Lianne's face just fell and she dropped her knife. "Of course, not…don't be silly…I…"

"Could you be pregnant?" Diane asked.

"I suppose it's a possibility. I am late, but just assumed it was nerves. OMG? What am I going to do?"

"OK. Let's calm down," Diane said. "We'll get a test while we're out and check. If you are it wouldn't be the end of the world, would it."

"Well, it's not what we planned, we said we'd wait a couple of years."

"And I don't suppose your Mam and Alfonso ever planned you, and look how that turned out!"

"Oh, this is so exciting!" shrieked Gemma, "a wedding and a baby!"

Diane tried to calm both Lianne and Gemma by reiterating that they knew nothing for certain and it could just be the stress of the wedding. Eventually she managed to get them both ready for their day out in Lucca and they all climbed into the car.

"I've been thinking," Lianne said as they drove off, "I don't want the day to be overshadowed by things, so I'm not going to do the test until we get back this afternoon. There's so much I want to show you, and I know you've been here before Gemma but there's still lots to see."

They all agreed that it was the sensible thing to do, even if Gemma was a little disappointed.

Lianne parked the car and they headed into the centre, there was so much she wanted to show Diane. The ice-cream parlour, the church where she would be married in a few days, the apartment where she'd stayed with Gemma two years ago, etc. It was a beautiful day, and a pleasant 21 degrees, so perfect for sightseeing. Diane was mesmerised by the architecture and the sheer beauty of the town; like the girls had been that first time she was overwhelmed by the aromas lingering in the air.

After a couple of hours, they found a cafe and stopped for a coffee and a piece of cake. Once again, Lianne ordered tea which seemed odd to the others, she'd always been a big coffee drinker and rarely drank tea, so this was definitely out of character.

As they sat in the April sunshine, Diane said she was so glad she'd come.

"Seeing all these places that you and your Mam talked about, is just bringing the whole thing to life. This is a beautiful place and I can see why you're happy here. I'm definitely going to have to come back and see a bit more of the country, maybe I can persuade a couple of the ladies from the bowls club to come too."

"That's an excellent idea," Lianne said. "I've only seen a small part of the country so far, but it really is beautiful. It reminds me a lot of Wales with the mountains and small valley towns. You'd love Barga, where Alfonso is from, it's high up in the mountains and absolutely breath-taking."

"I'd agree with that," Gemma said, "the drive up there is a bit scary, but it is definitely worth it. Anyway, ladies are we going to carry on with our guided tour?"

"Most definitely," Lianne replied. "I'll just pop into the pharmacy across the road first, and then we can head off."

The next few hours were spent viewing the many beautiful sites of Lucca, they even walked down by the river and enjoyed the gentle breeze that was blowing off the water. By about 4p.m., they were all exhausted and decide it was time to head back to the house. Once home, they sat in the garden in the shade and Lianne produced some homemade lemonade which was unlike anything they'd ever tasted. After an hour or so of general chit chat, Lianne decided she couldn't put it off any longer.

"Okay, I'm going to the bathroom!"

Diane and Gemma sat nervously and the 10 minutes or so that Lianne was gone seemed, like an eternity. Finally, she reappeared and was as white as a sheet!

"I'm pregnant," she stuttered, "shit, what am I going to do? What will Ricardo say?"

Diane stood up and hugged her, "You're going to be an amazing Mam and I'm sure Ricardo will be really excited!"

"OMG! I'm going to be an aunt," Gemma yelled, "this is amazing!"

Lianne could barely speak and she certainly couldn't think straight, then she suddenly piped up, "What if my wedding dress won't fit me?"

"Of course, it'll fit you," Diane assured her, "you're only a few weeks pregnant!"

They continued to chat about impending motherhood and tried to reassure Lianne until Ricardo arrived home, he said he hoped they'd had a good day and sat at the table, pouring himself a glass of lemonade.

"Everything is good?" He asked, "you all very quiet."

"Come on Gemma," Diane said. "I think we need to give Lianne and Ricardo some space."

They went inside, leaving them to talk. Gemma was desperate to eavesdrop, but Diane dragged her away. It wasn't long though before they heard Ricardo screaming something in Italian, and saw him dancing around the garden with Lianne in his arms.

"You're not cross with me?"

"Of course not, this amazing news. It must happen when you have antibiotics. I very happy, I be a Babbo!" With that he kissed her firmly on the lips and called for Diane and Gemma to join them. Ricardo found a bottle of Prosecco in the fridge which they duly drank, whilst Lianne stuck with more lemonade and the four of them talked incessantly about the baby that they knew would bring so much joy to their lives.

The following day was spent quietly sorting out some bits and pieces in the house, then in the evening the ladies headed off to meet Sofia and Isabella for a bite to eat. It was a lovely meal and thankfully no one questioned why Lianne wasn't drinking. Diane got on really well with Sofia and the two of them spent most of the evening talking about Lianne. Sofia wanted to know of Lianne's life growing up in Cardiff and about her Mam. She told Diane several times that Lianne was a wonderful person and that Lianne's Mam must have been incredibly proud of her daughter. Diane assured her that she was, and told Sofia about how wonderful Lianne had been when her Mam became ill.

"Lianne very special woman," Sofia said, "and my son very lucky to find such amazing wife."

"I think he's very lucky too," Diane said, "and I know they're going to be amazing parents."

It took a while for Sofia to realise what Diane had just said, and when she did, she stared at Lianne and her jaw dropped.

"You have bambino?" She asked, and as she did, so Isabella's ears pricked up too.

"Yes, I am. But it's very early, I'm only a few weeks pregnant, so still a very long way to go."

It was clear that Sofia and Isabella were overjoyed by the news and very happy, but Lianne kept playing it down, pointing out that it was still early days and she didn't want to say anything until she'd had her first scan. They all promised to keep the news to themselves for the time being, but Lianne strongly doubted that they would last 5 minutes!

Chapter 38

The night before the wedding, Ricardo popped back to the house briefly to pick up some bits and pieces before he headed to Sofia's where he would spend the night. Once he'd left, Lianne sorted out an evening meal for them all, before they went into full-blown pampering mode.

There were nails to be painted, face masks to apply, and unwanted hair to be epilated. The lounge looked more like a beauty salon and Gemma had bought the three of them robes to wear. It was a really fun evening; although there were a few tears as they reminisced there were also lots of laughs. Once all the tasks had been completed, they made their way bed for an early night.

It all felt very strange when Lianne climbed into bed knowing that Ricardo wouldn't be joining her, the bed suddenly felt very large and the room was too quiet. But Lianne was exhausted and it wasn't long before she was fast asleep.

When she woke the following morning, she could hardly believe it was her wedding day. The proposal seemed so long ago but in many respects it felt as if it was only yesterday. As she lay in bed, she could smell something cooking and so she headed downstairs to find Diane cooking breakfast.

"Very important that you and that baby have a proper breakfast today," she said.

Lianne sat at the table and within minutes Gemma joined her; Diane had made pancakes with scrambled egg and bacon. Lianne suddenly felt very hungry and tucked in, there was a fresh pot of tea to go with it and not a word was spoken until all three had been fed and watered! It was only then, that Lianne thought to check on the weather but she needn't have worried; it was a beautiful day with a clear blue sky and gentle breeze.

The night before, they had sorted out timings for everything and Lianne headed upstairs for a shower, Diane had already had hers and Gemma was also ready to shower.

"Off, you go you two," Diane said, "I shall clear up down here and let the caterers in, they're due in about 10 minutes."

Right on schedule, the caterers arrived loaded up with pre prepared canapés which went straight into the fridge. There were large platters of meats and cheeses, as well as several dishes which the chef would finish off in Lianne's ovens. Having ensured to the best of her ability that they knew what they were doing, Diane provided them with a table plan of where things were to be set out and then left them to it.

Upstairs both the girls had showered, and Gemma was styling Lianne's hair. Lianne had been adamant that she didn't want a professional makeup artist or hairdresser, she wanted to keep everything as natural as possible. The one concession had been a photographer, who arrived about half an hour after the caterer. Again, Lianne said she didn't want a lot of formal photos, rather a selection of more natural pictures, as friends and family enjoyed the day.

All three were nearly ready, when there was another knock at the door, it was Alfonso, and Diane said she would let him in, as Lianne wasn't quite dressed. As she opened the door, she saw a male version of Lianne standing in front of her.

"Come in, come in," she said, "I'm Lianne's aunt, Diane."

"And I am Alfonso! Lianne tell me much about you and I see you look a little like Maggie!"

"I shall take that as a complement," Diane said, blushing. "Lianne won't be long, she's nearly ready."

Diane and Alfonso continued to chat, and about 10 minutes later Lianne appeared at the top of the stairs, closely followed by Gemma. Alfonso was stunned when he saw her, she looked so beautiful and he was so proud to be able to call Lianne his daughter.

"Bellissima!" He said as a tear appeared in the corner of my eye. He embraced Lianne taking care not to smudge her makeup. "You look very beautiful and Ricardo is very lucky man!"

"Babbo, this is Gemma. My best friend." Gemma stepped forward, she was wearing a simple Grecian style, coral coloured dress and the most ridiculously high heels that Lianne had ever seen.

"I am thinking all Welsh women are very beautiful," he replied with a smile.

As Alfonso glanced down, he noticed that Lianne was wearing the silver and coral coloured bracelet that he had bought Maggie all those years ago, it prompted him to take a small box from his pocket and give it to Lianne. Inside was a pair of beautiful silver and coral earrings, they were very pretty and Lianne gasped when she saw them.

"I think you might wear your Mama's bracelet and so I wanted you to have something new to go with them."

"Oh Babbo, they are beautiful! I love them! Thank you so much!"

"Well," Diane said, "I think it's about time we made our way to the church." And with that, Lianne and Alfonso climbed into the car they had hired, and Diane and Gemma jumped into the waiting taxi.

Final Chapter

There are times in a person's life when they know something has happened which will change their life forever. This was one of those times. As the music started, Alfonso took Lianne's arm and led her down the aisle to where Ricardo stood waiting for her.

Who would have thought that her Mam's death and finding a few old letters would have led Lianne here, to this beautiful church, with the two most important men in her life, surrounded by her family and friends, both old and new, and with a new generation on the way.

THE END